Sheena is living the dream in the wilds of New Zealand: single, remote, self-sufficient. But as she finds herself in a world where haunting and inexplicable things have begun to happen, she's grateful to come across local Park Ranger Eric McRae, a sexy and enigmatic Scotsman. At first, he seems sceptical of Earth's imminent alien invasion, but McRae soon reveals he knows a lot more than Sheena could have possibly imagined. Her sexy Scottish lover turns out to be a matter-manipulating alien from another dimension, a species that is intent on fixing a broken Earth, and Sheena quickly discovers just how arousing first contact can be.

Out of Kilter

ISBN: 978-1-4874-4074-9
Cover art by Martine Jardin

Published by eXtasy Books Inc

Look for us online at:
www.eXtasybooks.com

Out of Kilter

By

NJ van Vugt

Chapter One

Sheena Bly regularly took her dog for a run in the foothills of the Waitakere ranges. Quimby was a particularly enthusiastic Doberman. He always raced ahead, came back a couple of minutes later to make sure she was still there, then ran on ahead again, repeatedly. Other than being unseasonably warm for autumn, this day was no different. Sheena followed her usual route, and Quimby followed his usual routine.

The dog had been gone a minute when she heard his barks. He sounded excited, so she picked up speed to find him. As soon as she joined him, the object of his excitement became clear. She drew her breath in, her heart skipping. He stood before a tree, just barking at it. Sheena had come this way not fifteen minutes before on the loop track, and this particular tree had been an impressive native kauri. Now it was no longer a tree of wood and leaves. The kauri tree had crystallized, as if the entire structure was made of clear white quartz. No wonder Quimby was yapping at it. She stared in disbelief. It was hauntingly beautiful. Sheena's instinct was to touch it, but she stopped herself at the last second. The crystalline structure just shouldn't be. She took a step back and got her phone out—no reception of course. She needed to go where she could make a call, but Quimby wasn't ready to leave. Sheena tugged on his collar to get him to move, and he still looked back and barked at the tree as they backtracked.

In the car park, Sheena opened the back of her car to let Quimby in, planning to drive further up the road where she might get reception. Before she had a chance to get in her car, a utility truck pulled in. The logo on the door told her it must be a council truck. A man in a ranger's uniform got out. He looked slightly older than her, maybe in his late twenties, and was tall, his handsome features enhanced by a smart goatee. She was a little self-conscious as she went up to him, still flushed and sweaty from running.

"I was just about to call for a park ranger."

"Seems I've saved you the trouble," he said as he put his ranger's hat on, covering his sandy brown hair.

She offered her hand. "Sheena."

He shook it and met her gaze. "McRae." His blue eyes were curious. "What was it you were going to call about?" He had an accent, but she couldn't place it yet.

"You have to see it to believe it. Something's happened to one of the big old kauri trees. I can take you to it, but do you mind if my dog comes?" She indicated the Doberman, waiting eagerly to get back into the forest. "His run was cut short."

McRae smiled and walked over to give Quimby a pat.

Sheena would have mentioned the dog was wary of strangers, especially males, but he seemed to indulge in the park ranger's attention.

"Don't see this breed too often. What a handsome boy. He's welcome to come. What's he called?"

"Quimby." Hearing his name, the dog leaped from the back of the car and shot off towards the track entrance. "He knows the way. We come here every week. It's our favourite track."

"Aye, it's a beautiful walk on a day like today. Don't usually get weather this hot in April."

"You're Scottish."

"Damn, I wish I'd known earlier, I'd have worn a kilt," McRae said playfully. Sheena laughed. It was a provoking mental image—an apparently well-built man in a kilt.

They followed Quimby as he sniffed his way along the

track, but it wasn't long before he ran on ahead.

"Tell me about this tree, Miss Sheena."

She liked him calling her that. "Well . . . this is going to sound weird, but it looks like it's turned into crystal." When McRae said nothing, she knew he thought she was nuts. "I *said* it was going to sound weird. You really do have to see it for yourself."

"Do you live local?"

"Close. Just along Scenic Drive. I'm renting a place there while I'm on hiatus."

"Hiatus?"

"I discovered recently that I'm not cut out for the rat race. I worked as a journalist for a few years but found city living so oppressive and stifling," Sheena said. "So I quit my job, sold most of the junk I'd accumulated, and moved out of the city and into the greenery. Now it's just me, Quimby, and nature. I have time and space to breathe, and the freedom to concentrate on what makes me happy."

"Sounds like you're living the dream. Not many people get to do that."

"Depends on what your dream is. Are you living the dream, McRae?"

He chuckled. "I suppose I'm living a version of it. I was a city lad, raised in Edinburgh. New Zealand always seemed verdant and remote and calm—a little self-contained paradise all its own. I knew I wanted to move here before I even started studying environmental science. I'm sure I made the right choice." Sheena enjoyed listening to his accent—the way he rolled his R's and pronounced certain words. It was almost magnetic.

Quimby's barks from further in the forest brought her back to reality. She and McRae jogged to catch up to the dog.

Sheena slowed as the ghostly tree came in to view, but the park ranger walked straight to it without hesitation. Taking his hat off, McRae wordlessly surveyed the crystalline tree from top to bottom. He tapped the glassy trunk with his pen, took a photo, then a scraping off it. He noted something down in a logbook. He was left-handed.

"When did you last walk this track, Miss Sheena?"

"About three days ago. The tree was normal then. It was normal when I passed it on the way down today. On the way back, it looked like this. I take it this isn't as freaky to you as it is to me."

He put his hat back on and met her eyes. "This is the second one I've seen personally, the third I've heard of in these ranges. Is this the only one you've seen?"

She nodded. "Do you know what would cause something like this?"

"I'll need to take these findings back to Head Office. I'd very much appreciate it if you didn't mention this to anyone. I don't want a stampede of curious people trampling through here. And it'd be best if you and Quimby found another track, for now."

He hadn't answered her question. She didn't at all like being kept in the dark. She held his gaze for a moment, hoping it'd prompt him to say more.

"Thank you for showing me," he said. "I can take it from here."

Sheena knew she was being asked to leave and reluctantly hooked the leash onto her dog's collar.

McRae pulled a business card from his breast pocket and held it out. "Call me if you come across any more crystallized trees, Miss Sheena."

She took the card and glanced at it. *Eric McRae (BSc) Park Ranger.* Sheena raised her eyes to meet his, and McRae tipped his hat—her cue to leave him to do his job.

Back home, Sheena did what she did best: research. A quick Google search and she found that similarly crystallized trees had been discovered in random places throughout the world, but only during the past two days. Scientists, geologists, and botanists had no idea what caused it. Intriguingly, testing had proven the composition of the quartz to be unlike any other found on Earth. Her interest was piqued, and she wanted to know more. She had a feeling McRae knew more. She needed a reason to see him again.

It was another two days before she came across a second crystalline tree, and Sheena eagerly called the number on McRae's business card. When he didn't answer, she left a message with her address and then waited.

Deeply involved in reading up on the Indian tobacco plantation crisis on her laptop, Sheena was dragged from her intense concentration by Quimby's *someone's here* bark. Just as well he was a keen guard dog, as she certainly hadn't heard the knock. It pleased her to see the outline of a tall man in a hat through the frosted glass in the front door. She took her hair tie out, letting her dark locks fall past her shoulders, and opened the door. McRae removed his hat with a smile and a nod.

"I got your message, Miss Sheena."

"Thanks for coming. I was kind of hoping you'd be wearing your kilt, though."

He chuckled. "Only on my days off." McRae gave the dog's head a good rub, and Quimby revelled in the attention. "So you've seen another tree on your walks, have you, boy?"

"Actually, I spotted it from out the back." She indicated for him to follow her. They went through the house and out onto the balcony.

"Got yourself quite a view here," he said as he took in the vista before him, down a tree-filled valley to the dam and back up. He leaned in to look through the telescope beside him. Sheena had left it pointed at the tree of crystal in the distance. McRae was silent, looking for quite some time. He straightened and turned to Sheena.

"What do you know about them?" he asked.

"I'm sure you know a lot more than I do."

"You're a journalist."

"*Was*," she reminded him. "These days I'm just a columnist."

"There's no difference. Your instinct is to research, whatever title you give yourself."

It was true, and Sheena realized she was dealing with a quite perspicacious man.

McRae indicated the kitchen table with her open laptop on it. "You tell me what you know, and I'll tell you what I know."

Sheena liked his offer. "It's a deal, on the condition we exchange information over a coffee?" He smiled with a nod and followed her back inside.

She handed him his coffee—black, no sugar—and sat opposite him at the table with her own cup.

"The first tree was discovered in Central Park four days ago," she told him. "It was attributed to an art movement or Eco group. No one's come forward. Since then, more have been discovered in different countries. Different types of trees, all sorts of environments, and the likelihood of it being a proactive or radical group is pretty small." Sheena held McRae's gaze for a few moments, but although he nodded, he didn't give away what he was thinking. "The composition of the quartz can't be matched to any other known crystal either, to add mystery to an enigma."

"It's not an art movement or an Eco group, this much I'm sure of," said McRae. "The soil around the trees hasn't been disturbed. We tried to dig up the first one we found. Every root, as deep as it goes, is crystal. What's happening is a natural phenomenon. Natural in the sense that every part of the tree itself has *metamorphosed* into crystal. It's not something manmade."

"So do you think this is nature?"

"Not at all. Nature doesn't behave this way."

"Do you have a theory?"

"I'm working on that. But *you* have a theory."

"What makes you say that?"

McRae kept her in suspense a moment, as he sipped at his coffee. He slid her laptop around so she could see the page she'd left up.

"I'd like to know what you think the connection might be," he said.

She smiled—he was genuinely interested. "Tobacco plantations have inexplicably begun to die worldwide, starting the same day the first crystalline tree was discovered, April 8th. Many, many cars just stopped, the first ones on April 8th, and no one has been able to make them start or explain why they stopped. The weather, in all corners of the globe, has been unpredictable these last few days. The date is the only connection I've made so far. Well, that and the fact that none of these occurrences can be explained."

McRae's gaze travelled her face for a moment. "*Do* you have a theory?" he asked.

"I wouldn't call it a theory. I'd call it . . . a conjecture."

McRae smiled as he sat back in his chair. "Go on."

"More unexplained occurrences will happen or be discovered until there's a definite connection. That's the journalist inside me hoping there's more to this than meets the eye. If I put a bit more effort in, I can guarantee I'll find something else related to the same date."

"Lots of things will have happened four days ago. Lots of things happen every day."

"I agree. But I don't know what's relevant and what's not

at the moment. Or maybe I'm just being hopeful there's something going on here."

"Am I having coffee with a conspiracy theorist, Miss Sheena?"

"No, Mr. McRae, but you are having coffee with someone looking for some excitement. Imagine if there are other forces at work, something otherworldly. Maybe this is their way of sending us a message."

"And what message would this be?"

"It could just be a wakeup call. Or what if these anomalies are all a side effect of something out there that we can't detect?" There was amusement on his face, and it made her smile. "I know, I'm a dreamer. Who am I having coffee with?"

"Someone who hopes you get the excitement you've been dreaming of." There was a pause. The way he'd held her eye as he spoke made Sheena wonder if they were still talking about the anomalies.

McRae finished his coffee and stood up. He put his ranger's hat back on. "I'm on the clock, so I should get back to work. I need to see if that tree you've spotted is on a walking track. It needs to be cordoned off if it is."

Sheena followed him to the front door. She was disappointed he had to leave. She wasn't big on visitors but really enjoyed his relaxed presence.

"Thanks for the coffee, Miss Sheena." He held her gaze, and her stomach fluttered. "Call me when you find some connection." She watched him walk to his utility truck and get in. She would definitely call him.

Chapter Two

Sheena kept a close eye on current events. The Internet was abuzz with crystalline trees and the pending tobacco shortage. Odd or unexplained things were happening every day. And there were definitely plenty of theories and speculation out there. She yearned for some proof that it was related to alien activity—but if there was any scientific evidence, it remained elusive.

It took her a few days to connect some dots, then she called Eric McRae, Park Ranger, once more. She left a message asking if he could stop by when next out her way.

Sheena was having a gossip on the phone with a friend when there came a knocking quite late that night. Quimby ran straight over to the door, eager to see who was there. Sheena opened the door with the phone still in her hand. McRae stood before her—in a kilt, no less. With his T-shirt revealing he worked out and his muscular calves on display, it was quite a remarkable sight. She made a mental note to find an answer to the age-old question of what Scotsmen wore under their kilts.

"I'll have to call you back," she told her friend before she hung up and put the phone aside. "I can't believe you actually own a kilt."

McRae laughed as he came inside. "In truth, I don't, and it wasn't as easy to find as you'd think."

"I'm flattered you tracked one down just for me." He followed her through to the lounge.

"I know it looks like I'm drinking alone," she said, a little abashed by the wine bottle and single glass on the coffee table. "But in my defence, I was having a Friday night phone catch-up with a girlfriend."

"I presume you own more than one glass?" McRae gave a cheeky grin that made her smile, and she went to fetch a second glass. When she returned to the lounge, she found that Quimby had rested his muzzle on McRae's lap, after some attention. The dog's head had pushed his green and blue tartan kilt up, revealing a fair bit of well-toned thigh.

Sheena tore her eyes away to focus on pouring two glasses of wine. "He's not usually such an attention seeker. Just push him off, if you like."

"I don't mind giving him a wee bit of attention. For a breed with a hostile reputation, he seems to be a bit of a softy."

"He's not normally that fussed with people, but he's really taken a liking to you." Sheena held out a glass. "Have you come across any more crystalline trees?"

"Aye, there've been quite a few more discoveries."

"What's the park's stance?"

"At first, they told us to keep the trees under wraps, to block off the tracks they were on, and keep the public out until we had an explanation. But now there's so many we don't have the manpower or resources to trawl the ranges to find them all. People like yourself are coming across them randomly. They've started to attract attention. The regional park's visitor centre has seen a massive increase in visitors over the last few days."

She found his accent almost hypnotic. "That's a good thing for the park, right?"

"It *would* be a good thing if all those people were coming to enjoy and learn about nature, and if they respected the tracks." McRae paused to take a drink. "But people are coming specifically to look for the crystal trees and aren't aware of what's around them. It's going to be destructive to the tracks eventually." Sheena heard the intensity in his words and liked how passionate he was about protecting the land he worked with.

Glass in hand, she sat beside him on the sofa and faced him, tucking her legs under her. "It's something to do with the environment."

"What is?"

"All the tobacco crops have died. *All* of them, every plant in every country. And there are major power outages in all sorts of places around the world, on and off since April 8th. There's been an increase in rain and unexplained weather. All types of vehicles have just stopped running for no mechanical reason. Not just cars, but trucks, buses, trains, and ships and planes, everything. They've been stopping since April 8th. You must have heard about some of this?"

"Aye, but I hadn't connected them to the environment. The government has been pushing for electric vehicles for some time. Don't you think it could be something they've masterminded and not connected to anything else?"

"It's *all* to do with the environment, if you think about it, McRae. There *is* something happening. And I think it's something significant. I think it's something we should be concerned about." Sheena watched his gaze travel her face, and she could see his mind ticking over.

"Go on," he said.

She smiled and sipped on her wine for a little while. "You're either a spiritual man, McRae, or a man of science. The signs could be viewed and interpreted from either perspective, or both."

He frowned at first, then a look of surprise crossed his face. "Are you talking about the *Apocalypse*?"

"There are murmurs of the Apocalypse from followers of faith, and rumours of alien intervention from followers of science. If these anomalies increase, it probably won't matter which you believe in the end."

"That's some conjecture," McRae said.

"I'm not the only one who's seen the connection; this is what the speculation is on the Internet."

"Do you always believe what you read on the Internet, Miss Sheena? As a journalist, I'm sure you're aware the truth is often stretched."

"Am I having wine with a sceptic?"

McRae gave a chuckle. "I've always seen myself as quite open-minded. I wouldn't say you're having wine with a sceptic so much as a realist." He looked at her as he again sipped his drink. "Who am *I* having wine with?"

"A journalist who's done nothing but research worldly anomalies all week. Reading about all these unexplained things happening does get the wheels of imagination turning."

"So you think we're experiencing an alien invasion? Do we need to make tinfoil hats?"

"Can you not take the piss for a moment?" Sheena asked.

"I'm not taking the piss. I'm asking if that's what you really think. Why would aliens turn random trees into quartz? Why would they stop cars from running, change the weather, and destroy the tobacco industry?"

"That's the million-dollar question, isn't it?"

McRae cleared his throat and changed position a little to face her better. "I agree everything seems to be connected to April eighth, but I don't think it's time to stock the bomb shelters or repent for our sins."

"I'm not going to stick my head in the sand and hope it all goes away. If aliens *are* out there, I'd rather be prepared. I think I *am* prepared."

There was a pause. They'd seemed to come to an impasse where their opinions were concerned. It was time to change the subject.

"When did you come to New Zealand? Did you come over with your family?" Sheena asked.

"No, it was just me. I left when I was eighteen."

"So you're all alone over here?"

McRae smiled. "Don't confuse being alone with being lonely, Miss Sheena. You'd know how that works. You've chosen to live not only alone, but remote."

"I'm on hiatus. It's a . . . lifestyle detox, and it's only temporary. When I'm ready, I'll merge back into society."

"What's all that really about?" he asked, looking at her curiously. "You chucked in the city life and let go of your worldly possessions to live like a hermit surrounded by bush—there must have been a catalyst."

Sheena smiled as she lowered her eyes. "I'm not a hermit. I still visit people and have people over. I'm just enjoying my space and freedom. But you're right. There's always a catalyst for a lifestyle change. Mine was the realization that I was living a *normal* life and doing *normal* things. It didn't feel right, and it wasn't fulfilling. Normal doesn't suit everyone, McRae. Normal is just a word to describe the most *acceptable* part of a larger social spectrum." His nod told her he was listening. "Enough about me and my abnormal lifestyle. How about you tell me why you came over to New Zealand without your family?"

"I'm adopted. When I was eighteen, I decided to find out about my biological parents. Coincidentally, it led me to the country I had always felt the urge to be in. I came over here while following my roots . . . and I never went back. Actually, that's a lie. I did go back to Scotland a couple of years ago to climb Ben Nevis."

"Are you a mountaineer?"

"It's one of my hobbies."

That would explain his toned physique. Sheena found her focus had dropped back to his strong thighs. What *was* under that kilt?

"Quimby," Sheena said. The dog still had his head on McRae's lap, soaking up the continual attention. "Time for bed." His dark brown eyes opened, but he was reluctant to move. "Time for *bed*," she repeated.

Quimby stood up and padded over to his cushion in the corner of the lounge, where he flopped down with a bit of a grumble. It made her smile. She looked at McRae, who met and held her gaze quite firmly.

"You know, Miss Sheena"—he finished off his wine and put the glass aside—"if an attractive young lass gave *me* that order I wouldn't need to be told twice."

Her nipples tightened beneath her shirt, and her pulse quickened. That was an overt hint if ever she'd heard one. Her focus dropped from his eyes to his lips, and she was compelled to lean in. He smelled of vanilla. It was comforting and a little heady. When she pressed her mouth to his, McRae's lips parted instantly, his warm wet tongue sliding between them to touch hers. He rested his hands gently in her hair and, in return, she laid her hands on his chest. Her mind again drifted to what there was under that tartan kilt, and she moved her hands to rest them on his thighs. His tongue repeatedly rolled against hers, and he gave a heavy sigh into her mouth. His blatant excitement aroused her further. Sheena pulled back from the kiss just far enough that their eyes could meet. She inclined her head towards the bedroom door, McRae following her gaze.

When he looked back at her, she said, "Time for bed." He stood without hesitation. She watched him disappear into her room and joined him moments later.

CHAPTER THREE

Sheena stood beside her bed and watched with increasing readiness as McRae removed his boots and socks. The second he'd finished, she pushed him onto his back. She parted his legs and knelt between them, her focus on where the kilt ended above his knees. The anticipation of exposing what was underneath had been turning her on since he'd arrived. When she bent to kiss him, he grabbed her head in his hands, not hiding his keenness. The smell of vanilla was strong; it felt intoxicating—or maybe that was from the three wines she'd had.

After a moment, she sat up to rest a hand on each of his knees. As she slid her hands up his well-developed thighs, she pushed the blue and green tartan up. Her breath quickened; the atmosphere was ripe with suspense. Sheena pushed McRae's kilt up past his stomach, exposing his hard, naked cock. Her pupils dilated. She'd seen her fair share of cocks, but this was by far the thickest. The discovery further increased her desires; she wanted it inside her.

"Don't be shy, Miss Sheena," McRae said, gently resting a hand on the back of her head.

She wasn't shy—just pausing to drink in the sight of his inspiring erection as it lay along his flat stomach. Resisting the urge to dive in and give head, Sheena caressed his inner thigh, stroked his balls, and then leaned in to leisurely pleasure the base of his hard-on with her mouth. It forced a heavy sigh from McRae, the foreplay obviously tantalizing him as much as stimulating him. She grasped his stiff cock firmly and closed her mouth around the swollen head.

As she gave a good long suck, tasting the saltiness of him, her clitoris throbbed between her legs. McRae let out another heavy sigh, this one of satisfaction, both hands in her hair now. Sheena took one soft warm ball in her mouth, rolled it around gently for a moment, and then did the same to the other. McRae lifted his hips to indicate his tight cock needed attention. She slowly licked up the length and sucked gently on the engorged head again before sitting back. Removing her shirt and her bra, she watched his focus drop to her breasts. The bulbous flesh fit perfectly in her own hands as she cupped and squeezed them for his viewing pleasure. Sheena rolled her fully erect nipples between each thumb and fore-finger, as much for her own enjoyment as for his. When she slid both her jeans and panties off, McRae's gaze dropped lower to her shaven mound.

He sat as she straddled his solid thighs, his lips meeting hers in a hungry kiss. His tongue was hard and greedy against hers, testimony to his unabashed excitement. Sheena tugged at his T-shirt, and he helped her take it off. She pushed him back again and paused to admire his smooth, well-toned chest. His nipples were semi-hard; the left one was pierced, and it just begged to be sucked. With the tip of her tongue, she rubbed at it, then sucked and bit gently. The now rigid nipple and metal stud were so unusually sensual in her mouth. She licked and sucked again before moving across to give the right nipple the same treatment. When she reached over to her bedside drawer to take out a condom, McRae began to undo his kilt.

"Leave it on," Sheena said. Her request made him smirk. He took the condom from her hand and put it aside. She felt totally ready to use it right now, but McRae was obviously more inclined to take his time. He lay back and rested his hands on her hips, gently pulling her forward, indicating he wanted her to shift up. She shuffled up to his stomach, making him smile.

"All the way up, Miss Sheena," he said, tapping his bottom lip. She moved up further and knelt over his face. He gave her soft, bare pussy a few probing licks, exploring her, tasting her. Then he went straight for her clitoris. He was so on target she let out a gasp, grabbing the bedhead. McRae worked it, rubbing with his tongue right where it hummed. Sheena tried to keep still, but the exquisite things he was doing with his mouth forced her to arch her back, rock her hips a little, and whimper. The way he massaged her clit expertly with the tip of his hot tongue pushed her to the point of no return. She rode each wavelet of electric pleasure as it rolled repeatedly through her body, giving a helpless cry of utter ecstasy. As those waves subsided, she was a little stunned at how quickly McRae had brought her to a climax. And now she ached to have him inside her. Sheena shifted back down his body, grabbed the condom, and ripped it open. She'd never rolled one on as fast and eagerly as this time.

Taking McRae's rigid hard-on in her hand, she straddled him, easing the head in between her legs, and as she sat, the whole fat length slid in, making them both moan. His hands settled on her hips to help her rock rhythmically. With his cock rubbing deep inside her, each thrust of her hips sent ripples of warmth through her body. Sheena leaned in, laying her breasts to his chest, clinging to him as she ground her hips to his. The groan he gave made her nipples sting. McRae grabbed her arse and squeezed, digging his fingers in, helping her ride him. His accelerated breathing was close in her ear, and the sweet smell of vanilla that emanated from him was invigorating, spurring her on. She worked at it, inner pleasure growing, and soon she was so close it burned. His thick erection stimulated her almost overwhelmingly, even more so when he lifted his hips in time with her rhythmic grinding.

Sheena reached the aching peak as she fucked him and cried out at the power and satisfaction of another climax.

Her mouth found McRae's, and she kissed him voraciously in her post-orgasmic miasma. His arms were taut, his chest toned under her rapacious hands. Sheena moved back down to eagerly get his left nipple in her mouth again, loving the sensuality of the silver stud against her tongue. But McRae soon pushed her back. He turned her to kneel on all fours before him, lifted his kilt, and plunged his thick cock deep inside her again. He thrust, fast but steady, and the tingle of inner pleasure reignited inside her. She dropped her head and went with it, soaking up the intensely exciting sensation of being fucked by such a sexy man, his rhythm slowly increasing in speed and vigour.

The buzzing In her clit became too much to ignore, forcing her to move a hand between her legs. As she rubbed and McRae pumped deep and hard, she let out an almost constant whine of delight, highly stimulated inside and out. He grabbed one hip firmly, digging his fingers in. His other hand settled on the back of her head, pushing her face firmly down into the sheets. The dominant gesture stimulated her and made her moan. McRae responded with a grunt of frustration. He lost his steady rhythm. He fucked her roughly, breathless and deep, no longer able to keep his sheer eagerness at bay. Her clit pounded, and Sheena rubbed and pinched it until a burst of overwhelming white-hot pleasure compelled her to again call out. McRae grunted with effort behind her, sweating and right on the edge. She heard him draw in and hold his breath, his fingers digging into her flesh. The tightness of his grasp bordered on uncomfortable until he at last moaned in orgasmic relief. He relaxed and slowed, breathless, as his hands wandered her back and hips, touching and squeezing.

McRae finally stilled and caught his breath. He pulled her long black hair aside and leaned over to kiss her neck and shoulder. The after-play gave Sheena's numb body the warm fuzzies. When he withdrew, she lay flat on her stomach, and he pressed his damp, heavy body along hers. He continued to move his lips and tongue up her neck, kissing her ear, into which he breathed, "If the Apocalypse *is* coming, then this is what I want to be doing when it happens."

Sheena chuckled. "I'm more than happy to sin to the very end." She rolled underneath him, pulling his lips onto hers. They lay together, elated and content.

The unfamiliar sound of McRae's phone woke her. It was far too early in the morning to be awake, especially after a long night peppered with sex and subdued conversation. Sheena couldn't even open her eyes as he left the bed. By the time he reached his phone in the lounge, it'd stopped ringing. She couldn't work out what he was doing out there from the noises she heard, but he eventually called out that he was going to take a shower. When he came back into the bedroom, he was in his ranger's uniform.

"Hey, what happened to the kilt?" Sheena asked.

McRae gave a grin as he picked it and his T-shirt up off the floor. "I only wear it on my days off."

"Have you been called into work?"

"Aye, always on call on the weekends. It comes with the territory. The ranges don't close." He sat on the edge of the bed to pull his socks and boots on and then gave her messy hair a stroke. "Don't get up, Miss Sheena. I can see myself out."

"Will you come and see me again?"

"Of course. Who else would I want to be with when the world comes to an end?" he said playfully. She pushed him away, and he laughed as he stood. She heard him leave the house, but a few minutes later, he was back in her bedroom.

"Did you forget something?" she asked. The frown on his face made her sit up. "What?"

"My truck won't start." His words made Sheena uncomfortable. That anomaly was too close to home.

"My keys are on the kitchen table, if you want to take my car."

"You'll need your car. I'll call a tow truck."

"I don't need my car this weekend. Just bring it back when you're finished, and we'll sort your truck out then."

McRae nodded. This time before he left, he leaned in to give her a kiss on the forehead.

Chapter Four

During the day, Sheena checked McRae's truck. It was dead, well and truly. She knew it was only a matter of time before her own car would be immobilized.

Later she gave in to her desire to read what had happened in the world overnight, knowing from recent experience that each day the news was worse. The smaller news items from throughout the week had now conglomerated into one disturbing international concern. Serious looting during blackouts, supply chain stoppages, major cigarette and tobacco thefts, unexpected weather patterns, and massive global transport issues. The world was in chaos. And the countless crystal trees were turning black worldwide. It all unsettled her a great deal, especially the part where no one could explain any of it. The words "alien invasion" and "Apocalypse" had turned from whispers to actual theories. Then her Internet connection went out, and she couldn't reconnect. There was no reception on her phone either. Suddenly, she was isolated.

It wasn't long before the enormity of her seclusion crept in. For the first time in months, she yearned for the company of others. Sheena hooked a leash onto Quimby's collar, popped in her earphones for her iPod, and went for a run to block it all out. It worked. Where she lived, far removed from the humming metropolis, life was always slow and quiet. Sheena almost imagined it was just a normal day. The only car she saw was her own as she neared her house. McRae pulled up beside her and rolled the passenger window down. "Need a lift?"

"I'm good. I'm glad to see my car's still running. You may as well use it as long as you need it. You can let yourself in and make a head start on the coffees if you like," Sheena said.

He grinned at her suggestion and started to pull away. Her car stalled, then died. He held both hands palm up. "I didn't touch anything."

He turned the key. They heard only a click. No dashboard lights came on, and the ignition didn't even turn over. Sheena's heart sank. Being remote obviously didn't make her immune to whatever was happening. McRae got out, and they had no choice but to abandon the car on the side of the road. The walk back to her place was a sombre one.

As she opened the front door, Quimby pushed in first and ran straight through the house, barking excitedly at the back ranch slider. They could see why. The silver fern close against the right side of the balcony had crystallized. It definitely hadn't been that way earlier in the day.

McRae slowly ran his hand up the glassy white trunk and then turned to her. "The crystal trees are changing colour."

"I read about it earlier." She looked through the telescope, which was still pointed at one of the crystalline trees down in the valley. The tree had indeed turned from a glistening, transparent white to a dull, smoky grey. They went back inside, and Sheena closed the ranch slider behind her, uneasy about the tree being so close to the house.

"Any news from your work about this? Is it why you were called in this morning?" she asked.

"Aye, it's why I went in. They wanted me to test a crystal sample. The trees were just pure crystalline quartz before. Now they're full of impurities."

"Are they degrading?"

McRae shook his head. "I can't tell you what's happening, Miss Sheena. The trees are the least of my concerns. My truck won't start, my phone won't connect, *your* car won't start . . . your power's out." He indicated her microwave, which had no clock showing. "No offence, but I'm stuck out here in the middle of nowhere with you while fuck knows *what's* going on in the city. I'd rather be out there knowing how bad it really is and helping any way I can."

Sheena understood his frustration and admired his will to help. "If it's any consolation, I'm on tank water and gas out here, and I could live off what's in the pantry for a month." His stern expression didn't change. "I have a mountain bike. It's a lady's one, but you're welcome to use it to get home."

McRae took her hands in his, meeting her eye. "At this stage, I'd ride a pink tricycle with tassels on the handles if it meant I could get home."

"Hmm, somehow you managed to make that sound sexy," Sheena mused, and he chuckled, leaning in to give her forehead a kiss. At least she'd made his frown vanish.

After McRae left, Sheena realized how vulnerable she was, even with Quimby at her side. Without a phone or Internet, she had no way of contacting friends or family. She couldn't tell what was happening out there, and didn't know when, or even if, she'd see McRae again. It was time to bring out the old radio and hunt for some batteries.

It was like listening to the 1938 radio drama *War of the Worlds*. According to the broadcaster, it was pandemonium around the globe. There was now a worldwide blackout. Every form of transport powered by fossil fuels had ceased working altogether. Electric vehicles weren't able to charge due to blackouts. The weather was unpredictable and erratic. There was looting and rioting, chaos and anarchy, and even hunger and death. All this, plus the blackening of the crystal trees, had thrown whole nations into a panic. But still, there was no sign of "alien intervention," no confirmed sightings, no substantiated contact, and no actual proof there was an invasion.

Sheena left the radio on for the rest of the day to keep up with events. It comforted her to have the voices in the background. She'd enjoyed the freedom of being alone and removed from suburbia, until now. Now the isolation began seeping in. As the day closed, she took stock of her rations and survival items. That night, for the first time ever, she let Quimby sleep at the foot of her bed, although it didn't make sleep come any easier.

A clap of thunder woke her sometime in the early morning. She lay staring at the ceiling, wondering if she really wanted to get up to put the radio on. For quite some time, thunder boomed above, and lightning lit the room. But it never rained. By the time Sheena got up to let Quimby outside, the sky was clear. The silver fern tree beside the balcony had turned a foggy grey. The crystal tree at the end of the telescope was black. It looked like it was made from obsidian and was just as eerily beautiful as when it had been clear white.

Sheena made a cup of coffee and sipped it while a radio broadcaster brought her up to date with what was wrong in the world.

Everything. Everything was wrong, and still no one knew why. Without transport, the world had come to a complete standstill. People were abandoning their homes and moving en masse into churches, schools, and hospitals. They were scared of the black trees, scared of the total power shutdown, scared of the crazy weather, scared of the unknown. Everything Sheena heard brought home her isolation. Being alone wasn't fun anymore. She decided that she would pack as much as she could carry and walk for however long it took, be it hours or days, until she found a shelter with other people.

While she was packing, huge pebbles of hail came out of

nowhere and pelted the house and the ground. Quimby shot out of the bedroom, and Sheena followed to see where he was going. He stopped at the front door, barking excitedly. The door suddenly flew open, and McRae lurched in from the hailstorm. He was breathless, drenched, and slammed the door shut as he dumped his backpack. Their eyes locked, and Sheena was instantly safe.

"What a sight for sore eyes *you* are," she told him. She slid her arms around his neck and pulled him—as wet as he was—to her, kissing him particularly ardently for a moment, breathing in his comforting vanilla scent. She went to step back, but McRae tightened his arms around her waist, and the kiss continued. When he let her go, she met his eye. "What made you come back out to the middle of nowhere?"

"If anyone's prepared for the end of the world, it's you."

"Is it *really* ending, do you think?"

"No, of course it's not. I'd be very disappointed if a blackout and a freak hailstorm signalled the end of days. Personally, I'd want something a wee bit more cataclysmic. Maybe fiery pools of lava just bubbling up from underground or a sea of green fog suffocating everyone in its path. Ooh, I know, bottomless sinkholes randomly opening up beneath people's feet, swallowing them whole, and you never know when it's going to be your turn."

Sheena found herself smiling at his mockery even though it irked her, but she chose to stick with her gut feeling. "I think we're being invaded. The whole planet's shut down. Something's interfering with our technology and our progress. Something's interfering with our *planet*."

"It's not an invasion, Miss Sheena. If aliens were going to attack, do you think they'd be so drawn out and sneaky about it?"

"They're *aliens*, McRae. Maybe that's *exactly* how they go about conquering other worlds."

"Hmm, I didn't realise I was up against a sensationalist."

Sheena frowned, looking his handsome face over. He seemed so sure it wasn't an invasion, so sure she was wrong.

She dropped her arms from around his neck. "Maybe it's time you took this situation a bit more seriously, McRae. And maybe it's time you took *me* a bit more seriously."

"I've just cycled forty-three fucking kilometres here, some of that in hail, on a lady's bike, to make sure you're not alone out here while all this unexplained shite is going on, and you think I'm not taking you seriously? I think the real question might be, *are you taking* me *seriously*? I've been out there, Miss Sheena. There are no men from Mars, there's no invasion, there's no Apocalypse. There's just panic and confusion."

Sheena took his cold wet hands in hers, realising she'd missed the bigger picture. "I'm sorry, I've probably let my imagination run away from me. I'm starting to go stir-crazy out here. Thank you for coming back to protect me. I appreciate it more than you know." He gave a nod of acknowledgment.

"What's it like out there?" she asked.

"Like you'd expect in a crisis. Vehicles are abandoned everywhere. There's police and military presence on the main streets, for what it's worth. I didn't really feel safe, though. People are so unpredictable in a crisis." McRae gave a shiver.

Sheena squeezed his hand. "Go get a hot shower. You're freezing."

She watched as he removed his jacket and T-shirt on his way to the bathroom. The sight of his broad shoulders and burly back stirred up a deep desire to be with him.

The shower had been running for a minute when Sheena slipped into the bathroom, naked, and joined McRae under the water, more than ready to take her mind off what was happening.

"I thought you might like a hand warming up," she said, lathering her hands with the soap. He responded with a sexy smirk.

Running her hands up his chest, over his shoulders, then down his arms to the tip of his fingers, Sheena both washed and caressed his body at the same time. She turned him and slid her foamy hands from his broad shoulders, down the taper of his back to his solid backside. Slithering a hand between his thighs, she cupped and gently massaged his balls. As hoped, McRae gave a soft sigh of pleasure. After soaping her hands again, she knelt and slid both hands slowly but firmly down one strong thigh and then the other. His hardening cock was at eye level, but Sheena disregarded it for the time being. With a little more soap, she stroked his calves and then rubbed each foot, making sure no part of his body was neglected.

Staying on her knees, Sheena brushed her lips over his flat stomach, dipped her tongue in an out of his navel softly, and showered his abs with butterfly kisses. McRae rested his hands in her hair, soaking up the attention, the sensuality. She rolled her tongue around one of his balls, sucked it gently and then quite firmly, before doing the same to the other. Starting at the base of his hard-on, Sheena took her time licking all the way up the length once, twice, and thrice. Then she nuzzled his hard cock, enjoying the hot, elastic skin against her face. As she gave the swollen head a tender suck, Sheena breathed a moan of satisfaction. The engorged glans was a pleasure to have in her mouth, so she sucked for a while as McRae watched. Looking up, she saw that his eyelids were heavy in indulgence. She stood and brought her mouth to his pierced nipple. Her tongue rubbed repeatedly on the silver stud. Sliding her mouth across to his right nipple, Sheena lapped at it until it was fully erect and sheer pleasure to suckle on.

He took her head in his hands and pulled her lips to his, kissing her hungrily, exuberantly. Sheena delighted in how unashamed his kisses were, with plenty of hard tongue and heavy sighs. And she was beginning to adore the sweet scent of vanilla. He backed her against the wall and got down on his knees, his mouth covering her nipple, his tongue circling it. When he gave a particularly hard suckle, Sheena inhaled deeply at the satisfying sting. By the time he'd finished tonguing and sucking her nipples, they were stiff and burning.

McRae let his tongue lead the way downwards as he lifted her thigh over his shoulder. He spread her lips open with his thumbs and licked her exposed clitoris. Again, Sheena inhaled sharply, her hands settling in his wet hair. The tip of his tongue wriggled against the nub that'd been quietly buzzing in the background since she'd joined him in the shower, and the warmth of pleasure spread inside her. He changed his angle, pressed his tongue harder, and worked at her clit until she scrunched her fists in his hair, letting out a blissful cry. McRae firmly lapped right on her nub. Sheena could barely keep still, pressing herself into his mouth to make him stimulate her harder. He changed tactic once more, sucking on her sensitive clit in little pulses. Her pleasure peaked, and she moaned as she swam in a sea of orgasmic ecstasy.

As she came down, he slid his tongue inside her, thrusting it deep. Then McRae stood, pressing his body hard against hers, and hers hard against the wall.

After kissing her greedily for a moment, he whispered, "Tell me you brought a condom in with you."

"I brought a condom in with me. It's on the vanity." McRae turned to throw open the shower curtain. He grabbed the condom and paused to hastily roll it on. Then he turned and pressed Sheena back against the wall, lifting her. She wrapped her legs around him as he eased the swollen head of his rigid cock inside her, his hands firmly around her slim waist. He penetrated her deeply, a moment she'd very much been looking forward to. Sheena grabbed at the railings above her and lifted her weight off him as he thrust. Straight away, his hard-on touched her G-spot, and she gave a whine of delight.

His fingers dug into her hips, and McRae soon lost his steady rhythm in his excitement. He fucked her deeply, vigorously. The effort of his breathing became hard, the very audible quiver in his sighs a testament to his arousal. Sheena was disappointed when he stopped and withdrew, as she loved his roughness, his blatant horniness. He turned her around and bent her slightly as he placed her hands against the wall. He re-entered her from behind with a soft moan, and within seconds was fucking her fast and hard.

This position was instantly gratifying, McRae's thick erection ramming repeatedly against her sweet spot. He slid his hands up from her hips to her breasts and pinched both nipples. Her nipples burned with pleasurable pain, and she had to cry out. When he did it again, her clitoris began to throb. She dropped a hand and felt between her own legs. The pleasure welled rapidly as she stimulated herself, and it wasn't long before a white-hot wave of orgasm spread throughout her body. She tried to stand as she moaned, but McRae pushed her back over and held her hands to the wall as he fucked her roughly. She could hear his hard breathing now coming from between his teeth. She could hear he was holding off but right on the edge, in that place just between the aching pain of desperately needing to come, and the sweet release of orgasm. Her skin broke out in goose bumps at the deep groan of ecstasy he gave as he came.

McRae let out a long, satisfied moan as he thrust deep and slow, wallowing in the buzz from his orgasm. His tight grip on her hands loosened. Sheena turned and pressed her naked body hard against his, and they stood kissing under the water, their hands wandering as they came down.

She took her lips from his and met his gaze. "I'm not sure whether the world ended just then, but I'm damn sure the

Earth moved."

McRae gave a chuckle. "Give me half an hour, and we can make it move again."

"I like that plan. In the meantime, we should refuel. I make mean scrambled eggs."

Chapter Five

McRae ate twice as much and twice as fast as Sheena expected. The cycling and sex had sure worked up an appetite. She watched in amusement as he began on his third helping.

"Can I ask a personal question?"

"Aye," he nodded, pausing to sip his coffee.

"Any reason why you're single?"

"I'm not single." His statement took her aback slightly, and he smiled at the look on her face. "I thought *we* had something going," he clarified.

"All right, I left myself open to that one. Any reason you were single up until now?"

"Being single was a more recent status."

"Oh, have you just broken up with someone?" He nodded as he ate, and she left him to finish his eggs before asking, "Did you love her?"

After a short pause, McRae clarified. "Him."

"*Him*?" Sheena was more than a little surprised. "You were in love with another *man*?"

McRae pushed his empty plate aside, sat back with his coffee, and looked her in the eye. "Why do you say it like that?"

"Well . . . you just don't strike me as the . . . bisexual type."

"Type. Hmm. What is a bisexual type, Miss Sheena?"

She thought that one over. It was a good question. There was a bit of an awkward pause before she took his hand across the table.

"Sorry, I didn't mean anything by what I said. I don't have

a problem with your preferences. Making yourself happy should be a priority over everything else."

"I think I have a fair understanding of your ethics in life, Miss Sheena. Which is why I knew it wouldn't be a problem to tell you. There's no benefit in narrowing your choices down to one gender. Sex with a man or sex with a woman all results in the same pleasure, same emotions. If you're not limited to one sex or the other, then the whole world is open to enjoy."

"I guess I've never really thought of it that way. It makes sense, what you just said. Some people put a lot of importance on other people's preferences when they should just be minding their own business. Freedom of choice, right?"

McRae smiled. "You're a little bit different from the others."

"I've heard that before—but usually with a negative spin."

"Different is good." She was glad to hear him say that.

Sheena stood up with the plates, but McRae stood too, stopping her. "I'll clean up. You go and unpack. You don't need to go anywhere now. I'll stay here with you until . . ." He left his sentence unfinished.

After putting all her personal items away, Sheena switched the radio back on in the kitchen. McRae was messing around with Quimby on the balcony—they were best mates now. She wasn't really listening to what the voice from the radio was saying, as she was revisiting the earlier shower sex in her mind. But she tuned in when the broadcaster's tone became excited, and she turned the radio up. Quimby began to bark outside. The broadcast became patchy, so she only caught parts of the update.

" . . . have come in . . . see unidentified objects are . . . from the sky planet-wide. My God, I . . . being attacked . . . It's an invasion. I repeat: the invasion has started!"

Sheena dropped everything and ran to the balcony. "McRae, the invasion's . . ." She trailed off when she saw what

Quimby was barking at and what McRae was looking up at. Frequent flashes lit the cloud cover, each time just before an orange object fell from the sky. She and McRae watched in stunned silence as some dropped into the dam. The air was still and warm. There was an eerie silence in the valley, where there was usually a constant chorus of birdsong. Sheena grabbed the telescope to get a better look at their invaders. She could see an orange disc roughly the same shape and size as a surfboard floating in the dam. The water bubbled around it before it sank.

"Oh, God, what are they doing? Are they poisoning our water? Fuck, fuck, it must be chemical warfare," she cried.

McRae took the telescope from her and aimed it at the sky, watching another disc drop. "Don't assume the worst. It could be anything. They could just be sending in drones."

"Is that any better? Fuck, McRae, now is the exact time to assume the worst. What's wrong with you? Does this look friendly? The time for being an optimist is over. This is an invasion, whether you're ready to believe it or not."

Sheena ran back inside to hear what the radio had to say. Orange discs were falling into lakes, rivers, streams, and dams the world over. The illusive aliens were contaminating every fresh water source. It was a very underhand attack. McRae came to stand beside her, and she turned to hold him. He was everything she needed right now. He was strong and characteristically calm while her heart and head pounded in unison.

"I wanted this," she admitted, her face buried in his chest. "I always wanted this. I wanted the excitement of first contact. I *knew* we weren't alone in the universe. But I didn't want it to be like *this*. Aliens never took over our planet when I imagined it."

"Wait and see what they want before waving a white flag. There are endless possibilities as to what their motives or plans are. Testing one of those orange things is probably the best thing to do. Our experts will be onto it."

Sheena leaned back to look at his face, incredibly glad he was there, and that he was composed and realistic, as usual. She ran her thumb along his bristly jaw. "I always thought that if an alien race was advanced enough to make it to another solar system, then they'd also be intellectually advanced and not hostile. I thought if they were that smart, that evolved, that whatever problem their planet was having they'd have the knowledge and technology to fix it. And they wouldn't need to come and take someone else's planet by force."

"You'd think that, wouldn't you?" He grinned.

"How can you smile so easily when our planet is under attack?"

"*You* make me smile, Miss Sheena. Would you rather I run around in a panic, boarding up the windows and doors? Because I can do that. I'm handy with a hammer."

Sheena smiled despite herself. "Okay, now I'm paranoid that we need to board up the doors and windows." She pushed him back and went to check everything was closed and locked, then pulled all the curtains together. But she knew damn well if aliens wanted to get in, nothing she did would be an obstacle.

The last of the discs fell from the sky as evening rolled in. The birdsong returned, a breeze blew the still heat away, and a sense of serenity settled in. Sheena's unease subsided as she, McRae, and Quimby sat together in the lounge, listening to the radio by candlelight. The orange objects had been brought up from various places and were being tested. None had opened or exploded. No aliens, gases, or weapons had come out of them. Later, it was reported that the discs were not only of unknown material but also completely impenetrable. Further tests showed they were absorbing water rather than emitting anything. They listened through the night. McRae fell asleep on the couch not too long after midnight, but sleep didn't come to Sheena for a long time after that.

When Sheena opened her eyes, she was in bed with McRae asleep beside her. She hoped for a second that yesterday had just been a dream. She left the bedroom and went to peek out the curtains. The sky was a cloudless and brilliant blue, the birds were chirping, but the silver fern by the balcony was black. Quimby pushed against her, so she slid the ranch slider door open just wide enough for him to squeeze out. She fetched the radio from the lounge and turned it on while she put the kettle to boil.

The broadcaster was talking about how much pollution had decreased since all the transport had come to a halt, the upside of an otherwise damaging situation. The orange discs appeared to be filtering the water—not poisoning it. The weather had settled over the last twelve hours, too. There were no signs of an actual attack, but the world was still on full alert, still recovering from the shock and coping with the blackout. There were also absolutely no signs of *anything* unidentified outside Earth's atmosphere to explain where the orange discs had originated. Now there were whispers that it was an *inside job,* that the aliens were already among us.

Sheena stirred the drinks, lost in thought when a movement caught her eye. McRae was watching her with a funny little smile.

"I think you were right," she said.

"About what?"

She handed him his coffee and leaned on the kitchen bench with her own. "It's not an invasion."

"Is that what the general consensus is now?"

"There was never an actual attack."

"So those orange things last night?"

"Water filters, water purifiers. What if . . . what if the aliens have been *helping* us?"

"That's a change of direction from *help, help, we're being invaded!* Seems you wasted a perfectly good panic yesterday."

Sheena smiled with a shake of her head. "I think it was perfectly *justified* panic. We can't all be as cool, calm, and collected as you, McRae. Anyway"—she sipped her coffee—"they might already be among us."

He gave a frown. "Who?"

"Aliens."

"You think aliens are among us now?"

"I'm telling you what the speculation is. I *am* having coffee with a sceptic. You brush off every theory out there."

"Don't you think if the aliens were down here that someone would have noticed by now? Don't you think the International Space Station, or SETI, or at the very least one of the observatories would have seen something?"

"How do we know they can't camouflage themselves or . . . beam themselves through space? How do we know that they don't have some technology so incredibly advanced that we can't even begin to imagine what they're capable of?"

"Those are valid questions, Miss Sheena."

She rolled her eyes at not being taken seriously again.

While they drank their coffees in silence, the radio broadcaster talked about all the good that had risen from the ashes of Earth's recent turmoil. His sources had informed him that with all transport immobilised, carbon emissions, pollution, and smog had been drastically reduced. The crystalline trees were drawing in and trapping pollution from the air. The orange discs were drawing in and trapping water contaminants. The wild weather had rehydrated arid areas and refilled parched rivers. And although it would take years of study and testing to confirm, no doubt the death of the tobacco industry would ultimately benefit humanity's health overall.

Sheena saw how pleased McRae looked at hearing all this, nodding as he listened. She knew he appreciated the health of the environment, probably more than she did herself.

"It's not all rainbows and daisies, though, is it?" she said. "What's happened is going to be beneficial long-term, but the short-term fallout is we've now got a serious transport problem, a communications problem, and a blackout problem. Industry has ground to a halt. Where do we get commodities? A lot of people don't even have the basics. We're as good as back to the dark ages. I still need to somehow get to my family and friends."

"Let things settle a few days." McRae indicated the radio with his cup. "Keep an ear on what's happening. Are there any other stations broadcasting? This is only one man's report. Other people will have different versions of what's been happening."

That was something Sheena hadn't considered. She turned the tuner, coming across another station. A man and a woman were discussing the wrath of God, and that we as people had deserved this from Him for treating the planet He had created for us so badly. All those heathens were to blame, and it was too late for them to repent. Sheena looked at McRae, who rolled his eyes. She moved the dial around again.

" . . . and I have invited one such claimant into my home," a man was saying. "Now, you say you're an alien?"

"Actually, I said I was an Earth warden," was a woman's reply.

"What exactly is an Earth warden?"

"I feel I need to start at the beginning. And the question you asked starts at the end."

"By all means, start at the beginning."

"There were thousands of us conveyed here as babies and adopted out to human families. I lived a normal human life until I was about seventeen or eighteen, when I realized something was . . . calling. I had an overwhelming urge to find my biological parents. When I found them, they showed me who I really was, why I was here."

"I see. And what did you find out from them?"

"I'll start with why I was here," she told him. "I was cultivated to research and monitor the health of the planet. I gained a PhD in biochemistry so I could keep track of Earth's progress."

"So you've been feeding information from our planet back to yours like a spy?"

"Spy is a strong word, Mr. Blake. Spying suggests bad intentions, and we are only here to help. We've been monitoring Earth's problems a long time—you clearly don't know how to take care of your own planet, but you mean well as a juvenile species."

"That's a bit of an insult. So you think you're better than us?"

She ignored his comment. "We've been slowly gathering information to work out the best solution for your pollution and resource problems. And this month, we implemented it."

"Okay, let's say I believe everything you've just told me. So we've established your planet wants to help our planet. Wouldn't it have made more sense if all you *Earth wardens* maybe helped us discover a cure, or a solution, instead of the devious way you've gone about it? You've caused mass hysteria."

"Your problem is deeper than just your planet being out of kilter, Mr. Blake. Your *species* is out of kilter. If I was of a higher calling than Earth warden, if I was in a position to make rulings instead of data streaming, I would have your planet culled of the ignoble and selfish." There was a long pause, and Sheena looked at McRae. He just looked back without comment, without expression.

"She can't be for real," Sheena said. "Can she?"

"Are you asking me, who you recently accused of being a sceptic, if I believe this lady is really an alien?" was McRae's question.

"What if she *is*?"

"If she is, then we're lucky she was only cultivated to data stream and not to make rulings." That was an unsettling thought.

Mr. Blake continued his on-air questioning. "Okay, for those listening who might have just tuned in, I'm sitting with Nadia, who claims to be an alien raised in a human family. Her mission has been to provide her own planet with information on Earth's pollution problem, along with, what, thousands of others did you say? All this collective information has presumably been analysed, and a contingency plan devised to save us from ourselves."

"That's an accurate synopsis, Mr. Blake."

"So tell me why your planet has taken it upon itself to help us."

"All life is precious. There aren't as many life-harbouring planets out there as you might think—"

"I didn't think there were *any* until now," he interjected.

"Did you think in the vastness of space, the enormity of the Universe that Earth was the only one?"

"I'm not alone in that thinking."

"Have we not proved you wrong?"

"I haven't seen any actual proof that there are aliens here," he reminded her, then he added, "And it seems a bit of a coincidence that you look exactly like humans."

"This isn't my natural form."

"Okay, can you reveal your natural form?"

"I don't think you're quite ready for it. Ask me some more questions, and we'll come back to that."

"All right." There was silence from the radio as Mr. Blake

considered his next question. "Is there any way we can tell if someone's posing as an alien, since you're unwilling to show me what you really look like?"

"You won't be able to tell. We're all left-handed, but that's not particularly unusual. There's only one element we can't mask, and it's not something you'd pick up on."

"Can you tell me, or is that classified?"

"No, it's not classified, Mr. Blake. We emit a scent very similar to vanilla."

CHAPTER SIX

Sheena's blood drained from her face, and she took a step back from the kitchen bench. Her mind raced. With a hand to her mouth, she recalled snippets of information about McRae that fit the profile Nadia had described. She turned to face him and found him looking at her, silently.

"Don't be scared," he finally said.

"I . . . you . . ." She was lost for words.

"We're only here to help. But we're not a collective mind. She's alone in her desire to cull the planet; I don't agree with that at all. We're not invading. This is purely a rehabilitation program, Miss Sheena."

"You were . . . You said you were born in Scotland."

"Aye, I was raised there. I never said I was born there."

"You studied environmental science. You work for the National Park."

"With a cause to an end. I'm a data streamer, like all the others here."

"You knew about the crystal trees. You've known about everything all along."

"I never said otherwise."

Sheena tried to recall things he'd said in conversation, but her mind was swimming. He took a step closer, and she took a step back.

"You said you wanted first contact," he said. "This is first contact. Don't be scared." He was right. This was something she'd always wanted, something she'd fantasised about. But it wasn't exciting like she'd dreamed. It was chilling. She'd been deceived.

"You're not human," she said, and he gave no reply. "Show me your true form."

"You're not ready. You're already scared of me, and I look like something familiar."

"Of course I'm scared of you. You're an alien. You've been pretending to be a human. You've been using me for . . . God knows what purpose. Your species is insidious."

"I haven't been using you for any purpose," McRae insisted, frowning. "I've lived as a human for twenty-eight years. I've worked, I've made friends, I've travelled, and I've loved, just like you. I like it here. I like this way of life. And I like *you*."

Sheena saw the sincerity on his face and heard it in his words, but she was still shaken and wary. "This is hard to process."

"Aye, it would be. But I know you, you're open-minded, you'll make sense of this."

"I need a drink." She got herself a glass and randomly chose a bottle of red from the pantry. After filling her glass almost to the brim, she went to sit at the table to take a few much- needed sips. The glass was empty before it began to calm her. Sheena poured a second as McRae came to sit opposite her.

"Why did you come here?" she asked him.

"It wasn't a choice. I was cultivated. It's my purpose."

"No, why did you come *here* to my house."

"I like you, Miss Sheena. I like being with you, and I didn't want you to be alone out here when the water purifiers dropped. I knew it would be the thing that made people panic the most."

"You're right. Tell me about the crystallised trees. I take it turning them into crystal was an inside job?"

"Trees were chosen at random, implanted with . . . basically quartz spores. You don't have a word for it. I was coming to check on one of the trees I'd implanted when I met you."

"Did you implant that one?" She indicated the silver fern, and McRae nodded. "And they draw pollution out of the air?" He nodded again. Sheena took another drink of wine. "Did you stop my car?"

"No, that was controlled by changing the chemical structure of fossil fuels and ethanol. That's not my field."

"And the power cut? The weather?"

"Again, not my field. Electromagnetics. We have enough scientists and physicists and chemists to do most of this from the ground, with a little help from . . ." He indicated the ether.

"Do you have spaceships waiting out there?"

"We don't have ships. Um . . . it's not easy to explain. We're not corporeal, so we have no need for material structures. You could call us energy and matter manipulators. We assimilated your organic matter to take on human form. It's nice. I enjoy being tethered like this, having physicality," McRae said, looking at his hands.

"Oh God." Sheena knocked back her second glass. But she didn't pour another. Two before breakfast was enough even in this situation, and the alcohol was working. There was silence between them as she processed everything.

"Am I ready to see your natural form now?" she asked.

"I don't know, Miss Sheena. Are you?"

She breathed deeply, half exhilarated, half terrified. "Can you put Quimby outside?"

McRae got up, called the dog over, and gave him a good roughhousing before letting him outside. He came back in and stood before Sheena. Her heart drummed in her throat as she watched him close his eyes and exhale slowly. The air in the room became thick and warm. A fuzzy line appeared at his chest. It spread up to the top of his head and down to his bare feet. McRae's whole body caved inwards, drawn into that fuzzy line, like he was imploding. What was left was a blurry, six-foot streak that looked a lot like the blind spot she experienced during a migraine. For a moment, it was as if part of her vision was missing. The sweet and comforting aroma of vanilla filled her nostrils. Heat radiated from the distortion. It began to give off a faint, multihued glow, and then seemed to stabilise. Sheena stared at the unworldly spectre, still feeling a mixture of exhilaration and fear. He was as hauntingly beautiful as the trees of crystal.

Sheena was drawn to him. She cautiously put out a hand, and the warmth increased. Slowly, she let her fingers reach into the glow. Her skin prickled, and the hair on her arm stood on end. Touching an alien—she was touching an alien. First contact. It was the most extraordinary sensation. Sheena reached her other hand into the radiance and received the same static reaction. The allure intensified, and without hesitation, she moved her entire body into the distortion. Tingling warmth enveloped her and every hair on her body stood up. Every muscle gloriously relaxed, and she let herself go limp. Sheena's feet no longer touched the ground; she floated weightlessly, enclosed in radiance, inside McRae. His presence surrounded her, and with her eyes closed, she clearly saw his handsome face.

"You're beautiful," she whispered. The warmth seemed to tighten around her. It kept tightening, pulsating in waves around her whole body. It suffocated her. It burned on her skin until it penetrated her every pore. Now McRae was inside her. Each of her senses was heightened to the limit, and her body was wracked with the epitome of fleshly pleasure. Her skin was on fire. Her nipples ached like never before. Her clit throbbed unbearably. It all came to a peak, and she felt herself burst open, moaning at the total and overwhelming euphoria that followed. Sheena swooned, everything fading away.

She opened her eyes a crack. She now lay on the couch, and the corporeal version McRae sat on the floor beside her. It felt like coming out of an anaesthetic; her muscles ached, and her head swam. McRae handed her a glass of water, which she sat up slightly to take. She was parched and knocked the whole thing back.

"Are you feeling alright, Miss Sheena?"

"Mmm. I feel a bit like I've been hit by a freight train."

"I'm sorry. I've never merged with a human before. I was as gentle as possible, but I obviously need to work on it."

"Was it as good for you as it was for me?"

He chuckled. "It was good for me. It's not like organic sex. It's more of . . . an awakening of senses. We don't have genders. We just are. That's what I like about this form. I can choose my gender and experience both sides."

Sheena gave a little frown and sat up more, very intrigued. "You can choose your gender?"

"I was assigned as a male, and I've mostly been a male, but I've been a female . . . not bisexual, as you labelled it."

"Oh, so when you were in love with a man, you were a woman? Which do you prefer?"

"I don't have a preference. It's all the same. We've had this discussion before."

"It was under a different pretext." She looked his handsome face over. He was different now; *she* was different. Her initial fear of him had completely dissipated, replaced with serenity and trust. "What happens now?"

"Now I'm going to make us something to eat. You're probably as hungry as I am."

Sheena rested a hand on his arm, stopping him from getting up. "You know what I mean. Are you leaving the planet?"

"Our work here is far from finished, Miss Sheena."

"And when it is?"

"Then I'll have a choice to make."

He went to the kitchen and turned the radio up. The broadcaster said that the aliens had revealed themselves globally and didn't appear to be hostile. There was going to be a worldwide adjustment period. There was, of course, the distinct possibility of outrage and backlash against the aliens for interfering despite their good intentions. No one really liked change, even less so when it was forced upon them against their will.

In her heart, Sheena knew there would be rough times ahead for McRae. And she knew that she would do anything she could to protect him.

Part Two

Chapter Seven

A voice from the radio droned on about the alien revelation. Sheena couldn't concentrate on the words. She felt physically drained, aching even, yet her mind was awake and racing. The erotic merge with McRae's alien form replayed over and over, lucid in the forefront of her mind, until the craving to remerge became an almost unbearable headache.

McRae rattled around in the kitchen as she willed her sore body to move and forced herself off the couch and into the bathroom. Sheena stood under the cascade of cool water until the sharpness in her mind dampened and the throbbing in her muscles lessened. It took a long time.

Finally she turned off the shower and stepped out onto the mat. Standing in front of the mirror, she stared at her own naked body, pale and vulnerable. She would never feel the same about herself, her life, or her planet, and she vaguely mourned the oblivious and innocent girl she'd been just days earlier—before she'd met the alluring Scotsman, before he and his species had revealed their covert existence and their plans for Earth.

Sheena stepped closer to the mirror and looked into her green eyes. Something made her lean in for a closer look. Around both pupils was a band of gold that glowed so fiercely she stepped back in surprise. Grabbing a towel, Sheena rubbed her face dry, then the mirror, and met her reflection again. The rings of burning yellow remained, but the longer she stared, the fainter they appeared. Or was she just becoming used to the sight? Either way, it could only be something left over from merging with a matter-manipulating alien's natural form.

Sheena took a seat at the kitchen table with McRae when he finished making pancakes, but he barely knew which of her thousands of questions to start with. There was silence at first as she watched him eat ravenously.

"What's your species called? Do you have a spoken language, or do you communicate telepathically? How many of you are here on Earth? What's your home planet like?" The questions fell helplessly from her lips before she could stop them.

A look of amusement crossed McRae's face. "There are approximately eight hundred and forty thousand of us on Earth. We don't have a name for ourselves. We just are. But we are, by nature, wardens, as humans have named us. We don't have a language, and we don't communicate telepathically either. You don't have a word for it; it's more along the lines of data-wave exchanges. And we don't come from or live on a planet. We're from . . . you don't have a word for that either. You could probably liken it to a sub-dimension or maybe a *plane of existence*."

"You realize none of what you just said is something my simple human brain can comprehend, right?"

McRae chuckled, shaking his head a little. "The human brain's not as simple as you think. You just don't access it fully. And you don't need to for your level of being."

"Level of being. Hmm." Sheena felt vaguely offended. "Are you *ascended* beings?"

"No." He smiled at the question. "We didn't evolve from something; we always have been, and we always will be. We're a singularity that came into existence when the universe did, and we will cease to exist when the universe does."

"That's something else I can't comprehend. Are you saying you're immortal?"

"Mortality is a human word that can only be applied to linear existence, such as your own."

Sheena contemplated his reply for some time as she ate. "I'm guessing you're more advanced than I could even imagine. Your species must have the technology, or at least the ability to just fix Earth for us."

McRae gave a frown as he sat back with his coffee. "Fix Earth for you? What would that achieve?"

"What do you mean what would that achieve? This is your whole purpose, right? Our pollution problem would be fixed; our resource problem would be fixed. Anything that's out of kilter could be fixed. *That's* what would be achieved," Sheena said.

"Our purpose is not to fix your problems for you, Miss Sheena. Our purpose is to rehabilitate you, to show you how to do it yourselves, within your own means. Almost everything we've done so far has been achieved using human bodies, human capabilities, with Earth's own materials and elements. You need to learn how to fix your planet and maintain it yourselves," McRae stated. "Our purpose isn't to share technology or accelerate your progress. Tell me that's not what you're wanting."

"That's what people will be expecting, or hoping at the least."

"Believe me when I say you *cannot* take evolutionary shortcuts." His tone was stern as he held Sheena's gaze firmly. "We're not a universal cleanup crew. We're here to guide you in the right direction before it's too late."

"Surely you've lived among us long enough to know what we're like. You're in for a rude awakening if you think you won't be hounded for information, continuously interrogated, if you think you won't come up against resistance. Not everyone's going to be as happy as I am that you've come to save the day."

"We know what to expect."

"Do you? I think more people will be angry with you or scared of you than you realize."

"*Everyone* will be scared of us," McRae stated.

Sheena watched him finish his coffee, a daring question on her lips. "And should we be?" The brief silence that followed made her uncomfortable.

"That depends on what scares you, Miss Sheena. Everyone will be scared of us for different reasons. Most will be scared of what we can do, but some will be scared of what we'll uncover. We *know* there are inventions, discoveries, and cures at your fingertips that have been suppressed in the name of money, greed, or power. Humanity's core is rotten. And we *will* expose that. The corrupt and ignoble will be held accountable, and the suppressions will be lifted." He stood up with his empty plate and studied her face a moment. "Anyway, it's not *us* you should be scared of. We aren't the ones destroying ourselves and the only habitable planet we have. What you *should* be scared of is how ignorant your species is of how close you've come to self-destruction. Humans are on the brink of extinction. And worse, you're treating your planet like you've got somewhere else to live once this one's ruined."

She watched him take his plate into the kitchen and rinse it. His words would echo in her mind for a long time to come. McRae came back and stood beside her, and she looked at his handsome face. Every single thing about him was a factor unknown, yet she felt compelled to be with him. He gave her hair a stroke, and it tingled where he touched her. She wallowed in the moment.

"I should go, see what needs to be done, what I can help with," he said.

"Will you come back?"

"Is that a request or just a general enquiry?" he asked.

Sheena took his hand, feeling the hairs on her arm prickle,

and she gave two of his knuckles a butterfly kiss each.

"I'd like you to come back." The prospect of merging with his natural form again still nagged at her.

"Then I'll come back, but I don't know when. It might be a long time."

It was a strange and lonely stretch of time with just her faithful Doberman Quimby and the radio for company before the power at last came back on. With the power came phone connection and Internet, too. Both were instantly overloaded, so Sheena had to wait longer to be reconnected with friends and family. Then she rang and talked to everyone she'd worried about during the invasion, exchanging stories and thoughts with them. She told some about her new sexy Scottish lover—but neglected to mention McRae was one of the aliens.

Reconnecting to the Internet was an immense relief, and Sheena whiled away many hours catching up on global current events. She tried to start her car, where she had abandoned it on the side of the road. She knew it wouldn't start beforehand since the international transport standstill lived on. It would do so until a renewable and universal power source could be effectively harnessed, mass-produced, and distributed—something that was being feverishly worked on. The only transport mobilized was anything that ran on biofuel. She didn't know why she'd hoped her own petrol-driven car would somehow be exempt. She wasn't special just because she was sleeping with an alien.

As her mountain bike remained outside on the front porch, Sheena had to wonder what mode of transport McRae had used when he'd gone—and could only presume he'd *beamed* himself to wherever it was he went. She thought about him almost non-stop.

A few days after he'd left, she got herself organized and

took the long cycle into the nearest township. There were many more black crystal trees along the way than she'd expected to see, but she wasn't wary of them anymore. In Sheena's mind, their beauty was enhanced by their purpose. What wonder of nature could be more beautiful than a tree of exquisite ebony crystal whose sole purpose was to filter pollution from the atmosphere?

Most shops were closed, some even boarded up. But the superette was still open, albeit not very well stocked. The store was guarded. In fact, so was everyone she encountered; they seemed standoffish, maybe even suspicious. It occurred to her that no one was sure who was alien and who wasn't. That was going to be a long-term problem. Her research had revealed there was absolutely no scientific or medical way to tell human from alien. If an alien didn't want you to know, then you'd never know.

She cycled home with fewer supplies and less hope than she'd set out for, then settled in for another stretch of research.

The Internet was saturated with opinions, advice, speculation, and unsubstantiated facts. Sheena weeded out the irrelevant and possibly incorrect information to get to the truth she suspected. It took a lot of investigation before the picture became clear. The world had quickly divided in two: those who welcomed the wardens—as they were now internationally known—and wanted to do all they could to learn about them and work with them toward the common goal of a clean, green, and repaired planet; and those who hated, feared, or mistrusted the aliens.

And then there was a group within the latter division who despised not only the aliens, but the humans who were collaborating with them. They were the ones that concerned Sheena the most. And with the tobacco, plastics, and oil industries all but shut down, global tensions were running high for many more reasons.

Chapter Eight

Taking Quimby for a run along her favourite track was no longer an option for Sheena until her own car was mobilized again. So she took him around the local roads, not needing to keep an eye out for traffic. She felt good after her run, and her day was uplifted further when on her return home McRae was waiting on the front porch. It surprised her how hard her heart beat and how her groin tightened at the sight of him.

"You could've gone inside."

"I don't have a key," he said as he stood.

"I'm sure that's not a barrier for you."

"There is such a thing as abusing your privileges, even for our species, Miss Sheena."

She was pleased to hear it, although she already suspected he was respectful, even a little righteous. She unlocked the front door, and he and Quimby followed her in. Sheena went straight for a much-needed shower—the overwhelming urge to merge with McRae had returned and hammered relentlessly inside her brain.

When finished and in just her bathrobe, Sheena saw McRae was on the couch with a coffee, Quimby's muzzle on his lap. The TV was on. A new twenty-four-hour news broadcast called Warden Watch now aired, keeping viewers up to date with all things alien, with a running commentary on every world issue their arrival had affected—good or bad. Sheena called Quimby over and gave the dog a pig's ear from the pantry, then shut the ranch slider once he'd taken it outside to chew on.

"How bad is it out there?" She sat beside McRae—as close as she could get without totally smothering him.

"Haven't you been out at all since I left?"

"I did go out. I came across a paranoid town."

He held Sheena's gaze. "Mistrust is now a wee bit of a worldwide theme, I'm afraid."

"You caused that yourselves."

"Aye. But do you think it would be any different if we'd contacted you first and told you our plans? You wouldn't have trusted us anymore. In fact, we probably wouldn't have been given the chance to show you how much we can help you. You need persuading, not forcing."

Sheena considered that for a while. He could well be right. People would be dubious of the aliens' intentions regardless. It was human nature to be suspicious of something new or unknown.

"If someone asks if you're an alien, will you be honest, McRae?"

"That would depend on the situation. I could ask the same question of you."

She nodded, as she thought it over. "You're right. I haven't told anyone yet." She couldn't stop staring at his face; his blue eyes were full of amused curiosity. "What's happening with the crystal trees? They've all turned black. Once they're full, what happens to them?"

"The pollutants will break down and be neutralized, and over time, the crystal will become clear again, ready to draw in more. It's a long-term, self-sufficient solution. The crystal trees are here to stay."

"The anti-aliens want to chop the trees down."

"Aye, there's evidence of that already. It's an exercise in futility, Miss Sheena. They'll still function as atmospheric filters whether they're standing or fallen. They're not going to be damaged or die from being cut down; they're not living structures anymore. And for every crystal tree that gets crushed into dust—which is the only way to stop them functioning—there will be someone like me to implant another tree with crystal spores." McRae sat forward and took her hands in his as he met her gaze. "As I said before, we know what to expect. This isn't the first planet my species have helped pull back from the brink of ruin. Whether the inhabitants are carbon-based, or copper-based, whether they're air-breathing or aquatic . . . whatever species they are they still split into the accepting and the unaccepting."

As he spoke Sheena felt the blood surging around her body, a relentless pounding between her legs, and her nipples were so tight they hurt. The desire to merge, which had simmered in the back of her mind for the last few days, now screamed inside her head like a migraine. She attempted to ignore her instinct to throw herself at him in a fit of frenzied excitement by asking more questions.

"Have there been times when the majority of a species didn't want your help?"

"No. There're always more for it than against it, in the end. It takes time for us to vindicate ourselves." McRae gave a frown. "Are you feeling all right?"

"No, I'm not actually. I don't know what you've done to me, McRae, but I've had a constant headache and felt horny as hell since you merged with me last week." She indicated his hands that held hers. "And every time you touch me, it gets worse."

A sexy little smirk touched his lips. He let go of her hands and tugged his T-shirt off, then threw it aside. The tingle began between her legs grew in intensity at the sight of his bare chest, at the thought of what was to come.

McRae laid Sheena back along the couch. He pulled at the

ties around her waist and pushed open each side of her bathrobe, exposing her breasts. Her chest heaved a little in anticipation, and his focus shifted to her achingly erect nipples. He cupped both breasts, closing his hands around them, and Sheena drew her breath in sharply at his particularly firm touch. Within seconds, he had one of her stiff nipples in his mouth. Having it so greedily sucked forced a gasp of enjoyment from her. He bit softly, and she pulled his hair, arching her back at the pleasurable pain. His mouth slid across to her other breast, and he keenly lapped at that hard nub, too, at the same time resting a hand between her parted legs. McRae gave a heavy sigh, his breath hot on her skin. She was so wet and ready that his two fingers easily slid into her, pressing straight into her sweet spot. As he thrust them deeply, still suckling her burning nipple, she pushed on his head. More than willing to oblige, he kissed down her body.

Goosebumps washed over her skin, and it prickled every place his lips and tongue touched. In dire need of some alleviation, Sheena pushed harder on his head, giving him the hint not to take his time. Her clitoris was swollen and clearly visible, making his next move a lot easier. McRae pressed his tongue firmly against it, and again, Sheena yanked on his hair with a groan of frustration. Within moments, he needed to take her hips in both hands in an attempt to keep her still. He continued to rub his tongue purposefully against her engorged clitoris, as constant noises of delight escaped her. He glanced up when she gave a particularly sharp inhalation. Sheena squeezed her own breasts and pinched quite roughly at her enflamed nipples, very much enjoying the relief it gave her.

He drew her clit firmly into his mouth to suckle on it. Her whole body stiffened. She dropped her hands to his head and tugged hard on his hair as she cried out. McRae continued stimulating her as she moaned throughout her much-needed orgasm. He then thrust his tongue deep into her, letting out a murmur. Shifting up, he lay along her, kissing her hungrily, and he hastily undid his jeans. Sheena ached to have him inside her and, at the same time, ached to be inside him. Her climax had not satisfied her the way it normally would have. She pushed his face back, her eyes locking with his.

"Merge with me," she urged.

"Don't be in such a rush, Miss Sheena. This isn't a race," he whispered. Then he pressed his lips back to hers.

He kissed her fiercely yet briefly and then sat up to pull his wallet from his pocket. Sheena waited a little impatiently for him to open and roll on a condom. As he knelt on the couch between her legs, he pushed her knees to her chest and leaned in, his mouth again covering hers. He licked excitedly at her tongue while penetrating her primed pussy. As he sank his rigid cock deep inside her, she linked her legs tightly around his back. McRae took it slowly for barely a handful of seconds before he started fucking her hard at which she whimpered. He lay his chest along hers, taking her hands in his to hold both arms down above her head. The air thickened around them, and he let out a long, low moan.

Sheena's skin tingled and prickled. Each hair stood erect, heat blossoming between their bodies. McRae's human form melted into a hazy alien aura, which enveloped her. Her body became ethereal, and as she lay weightless inside him, his radiance constricted and stifled her. He pulsated around her. Each pulse tightened more than the last and burned that little bit more, at the same time increasing in pleasure, until McRae's alien life force was within her. With her mind more lucid than ever, her body awoke with erotic cognizance. The level of lust she felt was close to unbearable. And as they lay as one pulsing, interspecies amalgamation, Sheena's very soul reached a state of suspended orgasm—she could no longer feel any part of her body. Her ears rang, and a sharp flash behind her eyes caused her to gasp.

A sense of falling made her jar. Sheena felt faint and weak, but she didn't black out this time. She became aware she was lying back along the couch. McRae's heavy and semi-dressed body materialized along hers, his mouth covering her mouth, the sweet smell of vanilla strong in the air. His steel-hard cock was still inside her, and he resumed thrusting. She slid her hands down to grab and squeeze his ass as he pumped. She slid one hand farther, cupping his balls. Almost instantly, he ejaculated with a deep and sexy groan. McRae brought his mouth to hers, and he French kissed her ravenously, breathlessly, his heart thumping in his chest against hers. When his excitement began to dwindle, Sheena gathered the energy to push on his shoulders, and he willingly shifted down. Splaying her lips open with his thumbs, his tongue instantly hit on her unsatisfied clit. After a few hard pokes with the firm tip of his tongue, McRae drew her clit into his mouth and sucked with intent. Sheena lay moaning from the spasms his hot mouth forced through her until her needs were satisfied at last. He licked the whole of her tenderly a moment as she lay numb and breathless.

"That was a new record. Naught to orgasm in under thirty seconds," he teased. He shifted back up her body, and a look of surprise crossed his face. "Your eyes have changed. They're . . . glowing."

"That happened the first time we merged too. It must be something left over from whatever you just did."

"That was a joint effort, Miss Sheena," he said. "You can still see all right?"

"Everything's . . . sharper, like there's more detail," Sheena said. "Maybe it's how *you* see all the time?"

McRae withdrew, removed the condom, and shifted to a more comfortable position for her. "When I'm in this form, I see the same way all humans see, because my eyes are the same. They're exact replicas. My whole body is an anatomically precise, fully functioning replica of a human male."

"So you feel everything, just like a human?"

"Everything is one hundred percent physically and biologically the same. I need to eat, need to sleep. I sweat, piss, bleed . . . I could even have children. Many of us do. There's no difference at all between this body and the body of a natural human—other than I have a second form."

"That and the fact that you have knowledge of the universe, of time and space, that I'd probably struggle to understand," she pointed out. "When you're in your natural form . . . how do you see the world around you?"

McRae was quiet, perhaps thinking about how to explain it. "It's not sight as you know it; it's the perception of compositions."

"Can you dumb that down for me? Remember, I don't access my brain fully."

He gave a chuckle. "I see what things are made up of—their chemical, or elemental, or bio-molecular composition."

"That's not easy to imagine."

"I wish I could show you. It's beautiful."

"When you all get together in your natural form, can your species . . . amalgamate into one being?" Sheena asked.

"We unify. That's how we communicate. That's how we exchange information. But we don't become one being."

A knock at the door made Quimby bark from out back. Sheena and McRae exchanged glances as he got off her. She pulled her bathrobe together.

"I'm not expecting anyone," she said.

"I'll see who it is, Miss Sheena. You're not dressed."

He did his jeans up, grabbed his T-shirt, and put it on as he walked to the front door, and Sheena went to make herself presentable. While she hurriedly pulled on some clothes,

McRae came into the bedroom.

"You have a girlfriend called Toni? Blonde, very chatty, double D's."

His description made her smile. "Yep, that sounds like Toni. Can't imagine how she got here."

"Your eyes, they're still shining. It's quite noticeable."

"We can sit out on the balcony. I'll put some sunglasses on. Let her know I'll be right there."

CHAPTER NINE

It seemed McRae was the perfect host. When Sheena joined him and Toni out in the sun, they were relaxing back in their lounge chairs, sunglasses on, already sharing a bottle of wine and discussing the recent events.

"I like your new housekeeper, Sheena," Toni said.

Sheena laughed as she took a seat. "Yes, I keep him on for the dirty jobs," she said playfully. She smiled at the way McRae chuckled. "How did you get all the way out here, Toni? I'm guessing you need a place to stay?"

"I cycled here. Well, I pushed the bike a lot of the way, since so much of it was uphill. Why do you live so far out? Those hills are a killer. And there are so many of those crystal trees; it looks quite strange. Anyway, I left this morning; it's taken me all day. Man, are my legs going to be sore tomorrow. And yes, I think I will be needing a place to stay, if that's all right. It was my idea to open a wine. I hope you don't mind." Toni was always talkative, flitting from one thought to the next.

"Not at all. Are we celebrating or drowning our sorrows?"

"I'm not sure. I need your opinion on something." There was a slight pause before Toni looked at McRae. "Can I be rude and ask for some privacy? This is girl stuff that you probably won't want to hear."

McRae stood instantly. "I'll make myself useful in the kitchen then."

Sheena poured a glass of wine for herself, noticing what looked like thousands of tiny rainbow-hued fragments instead of the usual burgundy red liquid. What had the merge done to her? She rubbed her eyes a little beneath her sunglasses and then looked at her friend.

"What's happened?"

"Okay, I've known you a long time, Sheena. I'm pretty sure you're not going to judge me for this," Toni said quietly. "I've got a problem, and I need some advice."

"I'll do what I can. What's the problem?" Sheena sipped on her wine and waited in anticipation for what was most likely some good old girly gossip.

Toni leaned in, removing her sunglasses. Her eyes shone even in the sun, both pupils encircled with blazing gold.

Sheena let out a giggle before she could help herself and clapped a hand to her mouth to stifle it. "You've been having sex with an alien."

"Oh my God, how did you know?"

Sheena lifted her own sunglasses so Toni could see her eyes were in a similar state.

"McRae's an alien?" Toni guessed. "And you've been having sex with his true form?"

Sheena nodded to both questions.

"I've been seeing Miles for quite a few months, but I had no idea about him until he showed me what he really was the night those orange things came down. I was never scared; I've always felt safe with him. It was my idea to have sex with his true form—just to see. It's unbelievable; it's like being in another dimension. Well, you'd know. Anyway . . . I think I'm addicted, Sheena. When he's not around, I feel like I've got withdrawal symptoms."

"Do you mean the pounding headache and the overwhelming craving to merge again?"

"I've got that so bad right now, and . . . it's got so much worse since I got to your place."

Sheena indicated inside the house. "That could be because of McRae. He's probably giving off some undetectable alien vibe or something. Have you talked to Miles?"

"He's been out at sea a couple of days. I don't know how to get a hold of him when he's away; he rarely has reception. He's a marine biologist, so he's out water testing or something like that. You know me, the little details aren't important. I haven't talked to him about this. You're the only person I've talked to. You never know who's going to be against human—alien relationships. I came here because I knew you'd be open-minded. I'm so glad you've got the same problem as me—I don't feel so sordid now. I know other people are merging, as you put it, with the aliens."

"Let me get my laptop. There might be some information about this if other people have experienced what we've been experiencing."

Sheena knocked back her wine before going to get her laptop. At her request, McRae followed her back outside, but he didn't take a seat.

"Did you know about this side effect?" Toni asked him.

"No, I saw her eyes shining for the first time today. I didn't know it would happen. I need to look into this, Miss Sheena."

"Hang on a minute, let me see if there's any information here." Sheena typed in a few keywords. There was an expectant pause as she read what had popped up. "It's happened to a lot of people, both sexes, there's a whole load of blogs here . . . um . . . same headaches, same craving to remerge . . . same glow around the pupils . . . Oh, this person's written a lot . . . he says he's been merging with his alien partner for weeks—long before the rest of us knew they were here . . ." Sheena trailed off as she continued reading to herself.

"And?" McRae coaxed after a while.

Sheena sat back, meeting his eyes. "Did you know this was a possibility?"

"Did I know *what* was a possibility?"

"His blog says the vanilla scent you give off becomes an addictive pheromone after the initial merge, causing withdrawal symptoms that strengthen in the presence of *any* alien. He said he's begun to *see the composition of objects.*" Sheena turned the laptop to face him. "Are you going to stand there and tell me your species had no idea this would happen when you merged with us?"

McRae frowned deeply as he leaned in to read the blog for himself. "I didn't know any of this, Miss Sheena. But I'm going to find out as much as I can." As he took a step back, a blurry line appeared on his chest, which spread up to the top of his head and down to his feet. McRae's corporeal body appeared to cave inward, leaving just a fuzzy streak where he'd been standing. The streak hovered in situ, and then glowed for a second before it vanished. McRae had returned to his natural form and gone, leaving Sheena and Toni staring at each other.

Finally Toni spoke. "Do you think it was their plan all along?"

"What's your conspiracy theory?" Sheena asked, and her friend smiled a little.

"To make us all addicted, so we *need* them."

"I don't know. McRae said he didn't know anything about it. He may be selective with what information he gives out, but I've not known him to straight out lie."

"What if it's some plan he doesn't know about? There are two types of wardens—the rule makers and the data streamers. The data streamers were placed here and given a purpose, and maybe that's all they know. Maybe they genuinely think they're here to save us. But people like Miles and McRae could just be pawns in a master plan to take over Earth. They might not have a clue."

Sheena didn't like that speculation—she tried to always travel a path of optimism. The thought of her lover being used as a pawn left a very bitter taste in her mouth.

"My God, I hope you're wrong, Toni." Sheena poured herself another drink, filling the glass to the top.

Chapter Ten

In the dim glow from her lava lamp, Sheena stared up at the bedroom ceiling. She'd been in bed for what seemed like hours, but sweet slumber just didn't seem to be on the agenda. McRae hadn't returned, and not knowing why was driving her crazy. She couldn't bring herself to believe he was in on such an evil plan to take over the Earth. And she didn't want to believe he was being unwittingly used by his own species. First contact wasn't the romantic ideal she'd first thought. Now all first contact had done was divide a planet and complicate a life she'd put such effort into simplifying.

And above all else, the desire to feel his bare skin against her own, to feel his hard cock inside her, and to be inside him, plagued her incessantly. At the thought of McRae's naked and very desirable body, Sheena found her hand gently sliding down her body, where it came to rest on the soft warmth between her legs. Her mind's eye travelled down a vivid mental image of his well-toned chest and down his well-exercised abs to his thick hard-on. At the same time, her fingers caressed and stroked the smooth folds of her labia. She had learned from experience over the last few days that a bit of self-pleasure wouldn't alleviate the level of need she had inside her, but at least it might help her finally get some sleep.

Pushing the sheets down, Sheena petted herself for a few moments before slipping two fingers inside her moist hole. As she worked them, poking and rubbing them against her G-spot, she spread her legs, her free hand pinching her nipples in turn. It wasn't long before her affected breathing filled the room. She slid those two wet fingers up and pressed them to her ever-buzzing clit. She thoroughly enjoyed the attention she was giving herself, but it was interrupted by a dull flash in her bedroom doorway. McRae materialized from the light source, and there was an awkward silence at Sheena being caught in such a compromising position.

"It's your fault I've had to resort to this, McRae," she said. "I hope you're prepared to take full responsibility."

He chuckled, not hesitating to undo his jeans. "I'm happy to make restitution any way you like." She sat up to watch in sheer anticipation as he undressed and then beckoned him to stand beside the bed. Grasping his semi-erect cock, Sheena leaned forward to take as much of it as she could into her mouth, then sucked long and hard from base to tip. McRae pulled her hair back, holding it there. She knew that watching stimulated him, and the heavy sigh of pleasure he gave confirmed it, as she sucked him the same way again. By the end of the third suck, he was fully rigid with excitement. She rubbed the tip of her tongue into his slit before closing her mouth around the swollen crown. The noise of hunger she let out was a testament to how much she enjoyed giving head. She played with his soft, hot balls with her free hand and forced a long *mmm* from her Scottish lover.

Sheena kissed a trail up his abs, stopping to make oral love to his pierced nipple. Both the nipple and metal felt as good under her tongue as the many times she'd fantasized about it while he'd been gone. She took her kisses to the hollow of McRae's throat, dipping her tongue in repeatedly before continuing up his neck and along his bristled jaw. By the time their lips met, she was desperate for some of his hard tongue in her mouth. And she wasn't disappointed. Reluctantly tearing herself away from the kiss, Sheena turned to her bedside drawer to find a condom, opened it, and rolled it down the length of his more than ample erection.

Not needing any foreplay for herself, she got McRae to lie back on the bed. She straddled him, every inch of his cock sliding deep inside, pressing her G-spot, and forcing a moan from her. As she worked her hips, Sheena felt the much-anticipated spiciness of inner stimulation. McRae's hands settled around her breasts where his thumbs rubbed hard on each reddened nipple. They were already aching, and when he pinched them, the gratifying pain made her whine. She rode him harder still, trying desperately to reach that tantalizingly close orgasm. Opening her eyes, she found him staring at her face. He met her gaze, holding it firmly while she undulated on his cock. As the hot pleasure peaked, Sheena gripped his forearms, their eyes still locked, and she moaned in ecstasy at the intensity of his stare as she climaxed.

McRae sat, pressed his mouth to hers, forced his tongue in, and kissed her voraciously. Heat grew between their bodies, and the strong aroma of vanilla hung in the still air. Her skin prickled on every inch of her body, and her heart pounded as his alien radiance encompassed her. She couldn't wait to feel it constrict and stifle her body. His tight pulsing waves burned in an immensely erogenous way, and McRae's essence first enclosed and then filled her. Her mind and body became one with his. She could see his thoughts and feel his pleasure, and as she gave into that unfamiliar feeling, her body reached a pinnacle of both carnal and cerebral ecstasy.

She floated on a sea of full-body gratification one second and then was straddling McRae's corporeal body the next. He tipped her onto her back as he remained inside her, got her closed thighs between his own thighs, and pinned her arms down forcefully on the bed. As he fucked her, grunting with effort and excitement, the base of his cock ground against her throbbing clit. Sheena had never needed to come as badly as at that moment. She lifted her hips, forcing him to rub harder still, right where she needed it. She wanted to grab him somewhere, but the harder she pushed against his hold, the tighter his grip became. The power struggle turned them both on further, resulting in Sheena calling out as the pleasure spiked and spread outwards, rolling in waves through her whole body. Her orgasm was breathtakingly powerful, and surprisingly satisfying, and afterwards, she lay limp and willingly took the hammering from McRae. With his mouth close to her ear, he panted, so close, so ready. He fucked her vigorously, and then his grip on her tightened painfully as he moaned loudly, reaching his own much-needed orgasm.

With damp skin and a thudding heart, McRae stilled to catch his breath. He let go of her hands and shifted down to kiss her. There was no urgency now, and the kiss was long and lazy, his hands roaming gently. Sheena felt his sweaty skin become hotter still against hers, and when her hair prickled, she knew they were merging a second time. His true form smothered her and pulsed around her. She was momentarily suffocated, her skin scalded. The feeling gave way to pleasure once McRae was inside her, her sexual awareness reaching its peak. As her thoughts merged with his, she could hear herself moaning. Her lips tingled, her nipples ached, and her clit pulsated until it erupted in orgasm once again. McRae's alien entity remained inside her, pulsing and burning. There was a glare in her consciousness, and for a brief moment, she couldn't feel her body at all. There was nothing but thoughts she couldn't understand and images she didn't recognize—it was peaceful and wondrous. With a shudder, she was back on the bed, McRae's damp and heavy body along hers, and he lay still, breathing deeply.

Eventually he rolled off and chucked the condom aside.

"Is it just me, or does the merge get more intense each time?" Sheena asked. Her limbs were too heavy to move.

"Aye, it does. And it will."

With some effort, Sheena rolled onto her side and leaned up to look at his face. "Something I need to know?"

McRae breathed deeply and put an arm behind his head, gazing up at the ceiling. "Which version do you want?"

"What are my choices?"

"Sugar-coated, or the cold hard facts."

"Sugar-coated isn't my style. Nor is it yours. And you're worrying me."

He looked at her, raising his eyebrows at how intensely her eyes glowed. "How's your vision? Your eyes are worse than before."

"*My* questions now, your questions later," Sheena stated. Her comment got a grin from him.

"I exchanged data with quite a few others, and the information was consistent with all of them. This wasn't planned, Miss Sheena. There's no ulterior motive. We didn't know the scent would be addictive, and we didn't know there'd be side effects from merging with humans. We've merged with other species before, and nothing like this has ever happened. The problem's being researched fully."

He paused there.

It prompted Sheena to ask, "So what are the end results of the side effects? Can the addiction be reversed? And what happens if someone addicted to the scent chooses not to, or can't, merge again? This information is going to affect how people see your species. Is this discovery going to affect your purpose here? Or are you going to say *oops that went wrong, let's leave before it gets too messy*?"

"You're asking some extremely relevant questions."

"I know, McRae, it's my job."

"So, everything I've said since revealing myself has been on the record?"

"I'm not a reporter. I'm a journalist. Before you guys turned up to show us what humanity's doing to itself, I wrote columns. Green columns. Ecological articles. I'm still writing, but under a different pretext. And my columns don't have any reference to personal feelings or opinions. They're fact-based articles borne from hours of painstaking research. But what you said about there being suppressed discoveries and cures is all absolutely correct—I know it's happening. How many times have I had articles pulled before going to print because the subject's been too controversial or made too many people uncomfortable? And when you said the other day that these suppressions, this corruption, is at the core of our problems and your species plans to expose it . . . I realized that you're not here just to help rehabilitate the ecological side of things. You're trying to fix the social and political side of things as well. I think you've taken on something dangerous. And I think you've underestimated the full impact of what you're doing."

McRae tuned onto his side to face her and gave her messy, dark hair a stroke. "I like that you have such a clear understanding of what's going on. It makes things a lot easier for me. But I'm only a data streamer, Miss Sheena. I can't persuade the rule makers one way or the other. I can only pass on my findings and my recommendations. And the cold hard truth is we *will* have to harm a few hundred thousand to save a few billion. There is a bigger picture, bigger than anyone realizes."

She had to remind herself he was a matter-manipulating alien and, despite having spent twenty-eight years on Earth, he'd been cultivated and given a purpose; he wasn't living under his own free will as such.

"Your species is doing the universe's dirty work ultimately, if you're traveling through space and time, or whatever it is you do, searching out planets on the brink of ruin. Some people are even calling the wardens angels—heaven-sent to right the wrong."

McRae smiled. "That's a poetic way of looking at us."

"Anyway, back on topic. Tell me what you learned today."

"You mean before I came back and interrupted your solo performance?" he said.

She rolled her eyes at his cheeky grin. "You know that was your fault. I'm an addict now, and you're the drug."

"That's also a poetic way of looking at it. There are two things happening." McRae cleared his throat. "The vanilla scent has . . . a slight addictive property, so when you go a short while without it, that's when you get the headaches. That's the only true withdrawal symptom, and it's a minor detail in the big scheme of things. If you didn't come in contact with any of us for a while, your symptoms would wear off, and there's no long-term effect. Once we've gone, there'll be no further problems." He looked away for a moment, then met her eye again. "But the main issue that's happening is . . . when a human and a warden merge, there's a residue that clings to you. And that residue wants to . . . connect with more of its own species."

"This residue is what exactly?"

"It's like a thin film of our composition, a trace element of our essence. And it's . . . looking to unify with its own species—which is where that overwhelming desire to merge is coming from. It's not actually a desire for sex. That's just how your human body's interpreting it."

"So each time we merge, you leave a trace of yourself in me?" Sheena guessed. "And this little part of you is going to increase every time we merge . . . to what end?"

He gave a slight shake of his head. "It doesn't increase, it strengthens. But we don't know the end result. It's just something we need to monitor."

"We're humans, McRae, not science experiments. Don't brush this off like it's not important."

"Miss Sheena, it's not life-threatening and, therefore, secondary to what we've come here to achieve. Who knows, you might even find it has *benefits*."

There was a long pause of silence as she mentally ran over various outcomes, and McRae gave her time to think her own thoughts.

"I'm too tired to deal with this information right now."

She turned her back on him for some sleep. He shifted against her, spooning her. She soon heard the slow and steady breathing that told her he was asleep. But even though her body ached to sleep, Sheena's mind remained overactive long into the night.

CHAPTER ELEVEN

Coming out of an extremely deep, much-needed sleep, Sheena could make out voices from the lounge. Two males were talking. She listened but couldn't quite hear the conversation. Almost instantly, though, she felt the overwhelming desire to merge—it was a mental craving as much as a physical one. And it was an almost unwelcome feeling now she knew the reason behind it. She slipped into her bathrobe and stood in the lounge doorway. McRae was talking to a man she didn't recognize. His back was toward her, but he was taller and broader than McRae, with a headful of sandy blond curls.

"Good afternoon. I thought I'd leave you to sleep in," McRae said. As he spoke, the stranger turned to face her.

"You must be Sheena," he said. He held out his hand. "Miles. Toni talks about you often. I hope you don't mind me popping in unannounced."

"A friend of Toni's is a friend of mine," she assured him as she shook his hand. Static prickled the hairs on her arms and her nipples became instantly hard—an unsolicited reaction. The presence of two aliens was really going to test her willpower.

"I told you she was a good sort." Toni came in from the kitchen with a tray of coffee. "I've been making myself at home, Sheena."

"As you should. Ta." She took her cup and had a couple of sips, smiling to herself at how brightly Toni's eyes were shining, giving away that she and Miles had very recently merged. But Sheena's focus soon shifted to the well-toned chest she knew was hidden beneath McRae's T-shirt. She looked at his face. And as he held her gaze, the increasing buzz between her legs made her say, "I should go make my-self presentable."

A cold shower and some discreet self-pleasure helped take the edge off her urges, but once back out among the two men, the feelings returned with a vengeance. She joined them at the kitchen table for lunch and the remainder of her coffee and listened to their banter. Sheena smiled inwardly at how normal the scenario would have looked from the outside. But an underlying atmosphere and a gut feeling of something *not* being said niggled at her.

"Why do I have a pending sense of doom?" Her question stopped the conversation in its tracks, and all three looked at her.

"Things will get worse before they get better, they always do," Miles said.

"What things?" When no one answered, she looked at McRae expectantly.

"There have been some . . . incidents. As you know, they're calling people like you and Toni warden-mergers. Well . . . that's one of the more polite labels. Your eyes make you all easily identifiable, and there have been a few cases of your kind being attacked by alien-haters."

Sheena met and held his gaze. "Define *a few cases*. And define *attacked*."

"It's unlikely anyone's going to come out to somewhere as remote as this, Miss Sheena. The attacks have all happened in densely populated areas." It didn't escape her notice that McRae had as good as avoided the question. That wasn't an issue—she'd research it later.

"So there's no problem for me to take Quimby for a run this afternoon?"

"No one's going to attack a girl with a Doberman, Sheena," Toni said.

Sheena smiled. "That's true. Anyway, I thought we agreed not to sugarcoat anything, McRae."

"Aye, we did." He nodded.

"Are they attacking the warden-mergers because they genuinely despise us for sleeping with the enemy? Or is there some other reason?"

McRae glanced at Miles, pausing before he answered. "They think we're brainwashing you or recruiting you. They see you as weaker-minded humans."

"Recruiting us for what?"

"A lot of people still feel we're here to take over the world."

"Well, you haven't done a very good job of convincing us you're not," Sheena pointed out.

"We've decontaminated your water. We've sustainably purified your air. We've ensured the respiratory health of your future generation. In the short time we've been on your planet, we've already stopped many fish, insect, and animal species from going extinct. We're on the brink of a sustainable fuel source. And now we've begun unlocking closed minds and opening closed eyes with an aim to reach total international awareness," Miles said in earnest.

"And simultaneously, you've ruined our economy and divided our people. *Thousands* have already died due to lack of power, lack of communication and transport, and lack of basic services. People like Toni and I are carrying your residue inside us to who knows what end, and now we aren't even safe in our own communities."

"Humans are not the only life-form on this planet. You may be the dominant species currently, but you're ultimately transient. There was life long before your species evolved, and there will be life long after you're gone. Humans can wear the loss of a few hundred thousand where many other species can't. I would rather see a thousand lower species thrive than one self-important species dominate and suffocate all others." The silence that followed left Miles's words ringing in her ears.

"Not all of us are self-important," she told him. "From what I can see, the species with the most self-importance is the one that's come uninvited to someone else's planet, firmly believing that their way is the best way. What gives you the right to tell us how we should live? I totally agree that we're stifling our planet, but when it comes to us as a *people* you're doing more harm than good. The way you're going about this may have worked on other planets, but you're turning an already dysfunctional species against itself in the name of redemption. So you can go tell your rule makers thanks for the good intentions, but now would be a good time to fuck off back where you came from."

During the slightly stunned silence that followed, Sheena got up to grab Quimby's leash and left to take him for a run.

It was raining, but the cooling downpour felt good. The more she ran, and the farther away she got from the overwhelming alien pheromones, the less frustrated she became until she was a little remorseful of her unprovoked outburst. Halfway back home, the heavy rain became a thunderous deluge. Sheena took shelter under a large tree to wait for the weather to ease up. Quimby sniffed around in the wet undergrowth while she caught her breath and thought things over. McRae soon joined her from out of nowhere and sat cross-legged before her.

"Where did that come from? I didn't know you felt that way about us."

Sheena hung her head, a little uncomfortable, but he lifted her chin, and she was forced to meet his eyes.

"A month ago, I was living the dream, McRae. And I worked really hard and made a lot of sacrifices to get where I was. And now I have something alien inside me and won't even be able to go to the shops without worrying someone's going to attack me."

"It will get better, Miss Sheena. It just takes time. And like Miles said, it always gets worse before it gets better."

"McRae, I moved out here to escape the dysfunction, to escape the reality of what we were doing to ourselves. But my research told me we were starting to chip away at our ecological problems; we were starting to understand what needed to be done and how to do it."

"That's only because of *us,* Miss Sheena, the eight hundred and forty thousand of us who've been pushing you in the right direction for the last few years. You must realize that. What *you* were doing as a species before we arrived, no matter how good it was, was always going to be too little too late. Not enough of you understand or care to make any real difference."

Sheena felt that sting a little, but it was something she'd always known deep down. Not enough humans cared about Earth to make any real difference. It was the saddest reality of them all.

McRae took her hand and squeezed it tight. "You care enough for ten people, though, if that's any consolation."

"I wish it was. And don't touch me." She pulled her hand back. "You know what it does to me."

"Is that a problem?"

"It's not as much fun as it sounds, McRae, being overcome with an uncontrollable urge to merge every time an alien passes by. It's not funny. Anyway." She pushed herself to her feet. "I think I need to apologize to Miles. He probably thinks I told him to fuck off."

McRae also stood. "Aye, he was a bit surprised at what you said, since I've been telling him how well you understood our purpose."

"I do understand your purpose, McRae. But there seems to be a hell of a lot of negative side effects from your good intentions."

"We're working on all of them. I never said this was going to be easy, just worthwhile."

Again, he took her hand, and it gave her goosebumps. She tried to pull away, but his grip tightened.

"You're doing that on purpose now," Sheena complained.

"So I'm not allowed to hold my girlfriend's hand without having an ulterior motive?"

"I don't think you have an ulterior motive, but you really need to let go."

McRae dropped her hand instantly. Rain thundered down around them and steadily dripped on them from the branches above as they stood facing each other in uncomfortable silence.

"We've got a serious problem, McRae. You and I can never have a normal relationship. Aside from the fact you're an alien and may well take off back to whatever dimension you come from when you've fulfilled your purpose on Earth, we've got a major sexual dilemma," Sheena told him in all seriousness. "There's a piece of your alien residue inside me that constantly wants to merge, not just with you, with *any* alien. I don't want to get aroused every time I shake someone's hand, like with Miles this morning. I don't want to have sexual feelings for eight hundred and forty thousand other people. This problem the wardens have caused needs to be resolved above anything else. You need to go back to the rule makers and tell them to make fixing it a priority."

"I unified with other data streamers, all of them *human-mergers* like myself, while you were still asleep this morning. That's where I came across Miles. We tried to convince the rule makers to be more proactive than just monitoring the problem. But they don't see it as a priority."

"It may not be an ecological problem, and I know that's what you're ultimately here for. But it's a problem that the wardens have caused themselves. I can't see why issues caused by alien interference aren't seen as a priority. You *must* have some sort of directive governing interference?"

McRae lowered his eyes. "Our directive is *natural environment primary, inhabitants auxiliary.*" He raised his eyes to meet hers. "The human element will always be secondary to the health of the planet."

Chapter Twelve

To say that hearing humans were seen as secondary made Sheena unhappy was an understatement. She walked out from the shelter of the tree, into the downpour. The torrent of rain did nothing to wash off the betrayal she felt. Her romantic dream of first contact couldn't have been further away from the reality of it.

Sheena let Quimby run on ahead. He wanted to get out of the rain as fast as possible, and he knew the way home. McRae jogged to catch up to her and blocked her path.

"You know I don't see the human element as secondary, Miss Sheena. *None* of the data streamers do. The rule makers—"

"You're no different to the rule makers!" she stated. "You've only ever given me information on a need-to-know basis, McRae. The more I learn about the wardens, the less I like about them, good intentions aside. Whatever trust I had in you before today is seriously under review. I think you and Miles can go now. I don't want either of you around until—"

McRae grabbed her upper arms so firmly it stopped her mid-sentence. Steam rose from his blurring body, while Sheena's tingled as his glow encompassed her. His presence oppressed her, throbbed and burned against her skin as she became limp and weightless. There was no sensuality, no erotic pleasure, only a connection to McRae's being. He opened his mind fully, and everything he thought flowed through her.

She saw a jumble of images she didn't comprehend and felt

unfamiliar sensations and emotions. Her mind was filled to capacity with unfathomable knowledge and information. But at the core of it all, she connected with the wardens' deep-rooted desire to restore balance. Their compulsion to conserve nature—it drove them forward like an overpowering mandate. Although all life was equal, whether it be the humble amoeba or Homo Sapiens, the wardens weren't going to leave Earth until civilization and nature were in harmony, no matter what the cost to human society. Humans could withstand substantial losses better than most species and could rebuild a better life with the right tools and the right knowledge. It was going to happen with or without cooperation; the wardens had been doing it for millennia and were in their element.

McRae's purpose tethered itself to the residue that subsisted inside her, and her conscience awakened fully. They were merged for eternity in just a few seconds. As McRae withdrew his mind from hers, it became dark, and she was falling.

When Sheena opened her eyes, everything was too bright—all sharp colours and movement, and nothing made sense. She squeezed her eyes shut, and her head thumped unbearably. Her soaked clothing was cold against her skin, and her ears were overloaded with an assortment of noises.

"Miss Sheena? Miss Sheena?"

It was too loud. "Shh."

"They're not capable of processing our data waves, McRae. What made you think it would be a good idea?" She heard Miles' voice.

"Shh," Sheena repeated. "Shh."

"You've given her brain damage. She can't even form any words."

"She's not brain damaged, Miles, she's shushing you." It was Toni's voice. "Sheena? Are you all right?"

Sheena kept her eyes closed. "It's too bright and too loud. My head's thumping worse than the worst hangover I've ever had—and that takes some beating." A head rested heavily on her chest. She laid her hand on damp hair.

"I'm sorry," McRae said quietly. "I just wanted you to understand us."

She scrunched a hand in his short hair and dared to open her eyes a crack. Someone had pulled the drapes, and the room was darker now, but colours still swirled and bounced off everything she looked at. Her mind couldn't comprehend any of it.

"I don't know what I'm seeing. It doesn't make any sense."

McRae leaned up, and she could see the shape of his face, but it was just a mass of colours surrounded by tiny moving threads. Sheena focused harder, and his handsome face slowly emerged from the disorder. "You said seeing the composition of things was beautiful. But if that's how you see, it's a nightmare," she said.

McRae grinned and leaned in to give her a hard kiss on the lips.

"I was worried I'd overloaded your brain. I tried not to share too much, but I think I was a wee bit heavy-handed."

"I didn't understand much of what you showed me." She tried to sit up, but every muscle ached, so she stayed where she was.

Miles sat on the coffee table beside them. "The human brain isn't compatible. And it's not even remotely capable of processing that much information."

"I wasn't trying to pass on information. I was trying to pass on our ethos," McRae told him.

Sheena met and held his gaze, her eyes blazing. "I saw what you wanted me to see. I *felt* it. You need to show it to *everyone* so they can understand."

"We can't. McRae already overstepped the boundaries by

doing what he did." Miles said. "Imagine the chaos if we merged with seven billion humans. We're here to rehabilitate your people, not assimilate them."

Toni came to sit on the floor beside the couch and handed Sheena a glass of water. "McRae can't be the only warden who's shared his thoughts with a human."

"He isn't. But he is the first one who, apparently, hasn't caused any permanent brain damage in the process."

It took Sheena several days to recover. There was no mental damage—this she could tell for herself. But things had changed. Now when she touched McRae—or Miles, for that matter—she wasn't sexually aroused as such. It had become more of a psychosomatic desire. And each time she *did* merge with McRae, she felt spiritually satiated, for a short time at least. Each time they merged, her thoughts and his fused for a while, and she couldn't distinguish his memories and feelings from her own. They grew ever closer.

With their ethos firmly embedded in her mind and part of McRae's species permanently within her, it wasn't more than a couple of weeks before Sheena realized she could never be without him—or at least another warden. She was at their mercy, and in her columns, she began to vehemently advocate for the wardens.

Those wardens who had publicly revealed themselves—less than a third of the 840,000—had both support and backing from high places. The majority of the world's government and military departments had quickly recognized the benefits and prudence of working with the aliens rather than against them. Over time, it seemed there had become more for than against, as McRae said would happen. But the alien-haters still fervently made their opinions heard and felt across the globe. They were quite proactive, too, protesting, blocking, or interfering with progress and even undoing some of the good that had been done. They just couldn't see how self-defeating they were, that the more damage they did, the longer the wardens would need to be on Earth.

As this new subsistence with the wardens became the norm, Toni went back home with Miles, and McRae came and went, going back to his job as a park ranger, continuing on with his purpose as a covert data streamer. The hard part was behind them, and tangible progress began to unfurl.

There came the much-anticipated new fuel source, now mass-produced and readily available to all. Hydrogen-based—no more polluting fossil fuels, no more EV batteries with their colossal carbon footprints. Transport was mobilized. Earth began to rebuild its societies and industries and settled into its new way of life—which consisted of more acceptance of the wardens by the week, as their improvements started to emerge in all the right places, and suspicions and doubts were allayed. The only thing Sheena wasn't looking forward to was the day the wardens would decide their work was done, and she would be alone. She never wanted to be alone again.

CHAPTER THIRTEEN

Even before Sheena left her car after stopping in the driveway, she knew McRae had returned. She sensed his presence. Or rather, the alien residue that resided within her sensed his presence, causing her skin to prickle. She liked the feeling, especially when she hadn't seen him for a few days, as the feeling was accompanied by the anticipation of great sex.

He was waiting on the front porch for her. And he was in his kilt. Sheena's sudden intake of breath at the sight gave away that she was instantly aroused. She loved the anticipation of not knowing whether he was hard under the tartan. Dropping her grocery bag at the bottom stair, she stepped up and pressed herself against him.

"Hmm." She grumbled as she ran a hand up each of his well-toned thighs and gently brushed her thumbs over his inner thighs. "I hope you haven't been waiting too long for me."

"I knew you weren't far away, Miss Sheena. I could feel you coming."

"I hope you'll be saying that again in a few minutes."

McRae chuckled as he rested his hands in her hair, and he pulled her lips to his. As he kissed her with his customary hard tongue, Sheena slid her hand up farther beneath his kilt. Again she drew her breath in as she closed her fingers firmly around his seemingly ever-ready erection. She squeezed and tugged the hot supple skin, and his kisses became greedier still. Sheena sucked on his tongue for a moment, then knelt and lifted the blue and green tartan kilt to expose his rock-hardness.

McRae held his kilt back to watch her tongue repeatedly encircling the swollen head. She let out a soft *mmm* of enjoyment while she sucked, her free hand giving his balls some attention. But she didn't pleasure him for more than a minute—too impatient for her own need of stimulation. As she stood, Sheena slid her briefs off from under her dress.

He wasted no time in kneeling before her, hooking her leg over his shoulder. Spreading her open with his thumbs, McRae started by gently teasing her tingling clit with the tip of his tongue. The lack of hard and immediate stimulation frustrated Sheena, and she pushed her mound firmly against his mouth. Her plan didn't work. McRae pulled back and continued to tenderly tease her, forcing a complaint from her. Next, he pushed his tongue inside her and thrust it deeply, over and over, but it only served to make her clit swell further. After withdrawing his tongue, he resumed his gentle clit-tickling.

"Ohh, God, McRae, wearing that kilt doesn't give you the license to be such a clit-tease. Put me out of my misery," Sheena requested. She scrunched her hands in his hair and pushed herself hard to his mouth. With a noise of hunger, he gave her clit a much-anticipated firm suckle, and she gasped in pleasure with a good yank on his hair. McRae continually suckled right where she needed it. It was audibly obvious he enjoyed every second of it. The pleasure buzzed and throbbed and grew, her breath accelerating rapidly. He held her hips firmly in place as she began to squirm. Quite quickly, McRae brought Sheena to orgasm with his mouth, during which she gave a long whine of pure gratification. When he resumed tickling her clit with the tip of his tongue, it sent warm fizzy ripples through her body, and she whined again.

McRae stood and backed her up against the closed front door. After a short, greedy, and tongue-laden kiss, he stepped back slightly. From the sporran of his kilt, he produced a condom before opening and donning it. McRae lifted her against the door, and she wrapped her legs around him. As he penetrated her, Sheena grabbed his ass and yanked him hard against her, forcing him in as deep as he could go. Her nipples stiffened fully at the moan it brought from him. With her hands under his T-shirt, she clung to his shoulders as he slid an arm around her waist and began to fuck her. To her absolute delight, McRae didn't take it easy in the least, rough and horny as hell.

It quickly became a particularly hard and raw fuck, McRae holding nothing back as he constantly rammed his steel-hard cock in as deep as he could get it. Each time, he hit Sheena's G-spot, bringing her climax closer. When he put even more muscle in, she raked her nails along his shoulders. It brought a noise of pain from McRae that pushed Sheena off her plateau of pleasure and into a very vocal come. She was barely out the other side when he stopped and withdrew. McRae turned her, made her bend forward a little, and pressed her hands to the porch railing. He lifted and held her left leg aside and re-entered her, hands-free. Getting straight back into the same hard and fast pace, he grabbed her hip and dug his fingers in. Behind her, she could hear his staccato breathing between his teeth. Sheena caught a flash from the corner of her eye, and Miles materialized at the bottom of the steps. It took him a moment to realize what he was interrupting, then a look of surprise crossed his face, and he grinned.

"I see I've arrived a bit early."

As the air thickened and his corporeal body was drawn into a blurry streak, Sheena's skin tingled, and the alien residue inside her rushed to the fore.

"Merge with us!"

The words left her mouth before she even knew they were forming. The fuzzy streak of Miles hovered before them for a moment and then moved forward to envelop the lovers.

McRae had briefly stilled but resumed fucking her, and Sheena's pleasure was heightened by the burning and tightening of Miles's alien aura. They became weightless inside him, and as McRae continued to thrust, he groaned long and loud close behind her ear. She couldn't tell if he had reached a mental or physical come. It didn't matter. Miles's own excitement combined with and heightened theirs, and his and McRae's thoughts merged with Sheena's. She'd never felt so aroused, so high. Both sexually stimulated men were pressed against her—one physically and one psychologically; one rigid cock deep inside her pussy, one deep inside her conscience.

Her nipples ached painfully, as if they could burst open any second; her clit was engorged to its absolute limit, drumming hard enough she could feel it throughout her entire body. The excitement was overwhelming, and she dropped a hand to press two fingers to her swollen clitoris. McRae's stiff cock still rammed hard against her G-spot, and Miles' alien form squeezed around them until he was inside them both. He pulsated within them, and between clenched teeth, McRae let out a groan that left no doubt he'd reached a gloriously gratifying come. It pushed her to a mind-numbing peak—Sheena's pounding clitoris erupting, white-hot pleasure surging outwards. It lasted for eternity, and she moaned for eternity. She could no longer feel her body. She just was. For a brief moment, she, McRae, and Miles were connected by just their thoughts and feelings. She knew everything they knew. They knew everything she knew.

They were grounded again, breathing hard, sweating, and coming down. McRae tugged on her hair, forcing her head back, and he leaned in to kiss and lick her neck.

"Fuck," he whispered in her ear.

"I was just thinking the same thing."

He lowered her leg, and she turned to face him. He looked as dazed as she felt. Sheena slid her arms around his neck, keen for a little sensuous kissing to temper the seriously warm fuzzies she had. But she pulled back within moments, looking around. Neither of Miles's forms was to be seen.

"He wouldn't have wanted to outstay his welcome, but he'll be back soon. Toni's also coming over," McRae said. "Let's go inside. For some reason, my legs feel like jelly."

Standing under a cool shower washed away the sweat but not the high or the fresh memory. Merging with Miles while fucking McRae had raised the bar particularly high for any future sexual encounters. There was a continual buzz between her legs. She had a love-hate relationship with the feeling. Sheena detached the showerhead and gave herself some manual alleviation. But even after pleasuring herself to a silent orgasm, the buzz remained. Although it wasn't between her legs, it was throughout her body.

She could have slept two weeks solid, but first she needed to eat before she fainted. She eventually left the bathroom and found McRae, Miles, and Toni at the kitchen table with lunch laid out. She avoided eye contact with Miles and felt an intense stab of guilt that she'd not half an hour before merged with her good friend Toni's boyfriend. She would have to come clean sooner rather than later, but it could wait. Besides . . . it wasn't really sex they'd had with Miles, was it?

"This is a nice surprise. I wasn't expecting any visitors today," she lied. "What's the occasion?"

After a pause of anticipation, McRae spoke.

"I invited them over. We need to discuss something with you and Toni. I'll give you a prologue, Miss Sheena. Our species is like . . . a *Lego* set. We are all separate pieces but can combine to be one. We all have an individual conscience, but readily connect to any or all others." Sheena saw a slight smirk touch his lips and hoped she wasn't visibly blushing. "We can choose to be a rule maker or a data streamer. Both have their benefits, and both have their drawbacks. I have nearly always chosen to be a data streamer."

"Why?" Sheena questioned.

"I'll explain that another time. It's not relevant to what I'm telling you now." McRae ate a few mouthfuls of food before continuing. "Eight hundred and forty thousand separate consciences were suppressed and amalgamated into replicated human babies and dispersed throughout the planet between twenty-eight and thirty years ago, to grow up just like you or Toni. We didn't know, or should I say, we didn't *remember* we were wardens until the rule makers made contact and unified with us. We own these bodies, we *are* these bodies, but, as with everything, they're manipulated from matter so we can . . . disperse them or . . . bring them together at will." McRae looked at Miles. "Did you know this is the one hundred and forty-first time I've volunteered to data stream? Every time is so incredibly different from the last."

"I haven't kept count. But this has been one of the easier planets to help. And it's only taken thirty years to see results. Sometimes, it takes the best part of a century."

"You're leaving?" Sheena guessed. All three looked at her, and she couldn't hide the immense disappointment she felt.

"Eventually, but not just yet," McRae assured her.

"You don't have to justify it with your life story. I know you're only here to do a job, and I know that your purpose for being on Earth has pretty much been accomplished."

"I'm not trying to tell you I'm leaving, Miss Sheena. I'm leading up to what we really need to discuss. There's been some news on the long-term effects of merging. Does anyone want a coffee?"

"Are we going to need one?" Toni questioned.

"I can't answer that for you. But *I'm* going to have one."

"I'll do the honours," Miles said. He stood up. "Don't keep the girls in anticipation."

So McRae continued. "As you know, we've been monitoring the warden-mergers for a few months now. Each case is different, but the ultimate outcome will be the same."

"Can you explain whatever you're about to say in layman's terms?" Toni requested. "I can't follow your scientific gibberish."

"All right, I'll try not to use any gibberish." He grinned. "You and Miss Sheena have our residue inside you. It's always going to be there. You're always going to feel the need to merge if our species is near. Once we've left Earth, the symptoms will probably lessen, but none of it can be reversed. It's permanent."

"If you leave the residue when you merge with us, why can't you just take it back when you merge with us the next time?"

"It doesn't work like that, Toni; we don't have any control over it. It's not part of us anymore. It has your individual *self* in it." McRae looked at the blank expression on her face. "Okay, it's like this. Some plants you can propagate from a single leaf. Um . . . propagate means to reproduce or to breed. You have the original plant—that's me. You take off one leaf and plant it somewhere else, and from it grows a whole new plant—that's you."

"You mean we're pregnant?" Toni frowned.

"No. Well . . . no." McRae looked at Miles for some help.

"It is a form of breeding, but it's not like you're carrying a warden baby. It's just a member of our species living within you."

"That sounds a lot like pregnancy, Miles," Toni stated flatly.

"Is this how your species propagates?" Sheena asked. "You

break a little part of yourself off, and from it grows a new . . . person?"

"We don't propagate. We just are," McRae stated.

"From what you've just explained, that's not the case."

"Okay, we've never propagated *before*," he rephrased.

"So why now?"

"Well . . . that's the unknown here. Of all the species we've merged with, we've never reproduced our own kind with them. It's something to do with your bio-molecular makeup. It's not my field, so I don't know the details."

"So how do we remove this . . . warden inside us?"

"You can't remove it. It's not just inside you. It *is* you." McRae grabbed her hand across the table, holding her gaze intently. "You're no different from me now, Miss Sheena."

CHAPTER FOURTEEN

Sipping her coffee, Sheena took a few moments to get her head around what McRae had said.

"I think I'd know if I'd somehow become an alien," she stated glibly.

"Wait . . . is *that* what you're saying? We're not just carrying aliens. We *are* aliens?" Toni asked.

"In layman's terms," Miles confirmed. "That's what our research has concluded."

Sheena looked at McRae curiously. "How do you turn yourself from human to warden?"

"I think it, and it happens."

"Can you be *slightly* more specific?" she coaxed.

He gave a grin. "I can't be more specific, Miss Sheena. That's like asking how do you walk, or write, or speak. It's an automatic response to a desire."

"So, in theory, I should just have a desire to change from human to warden, and it should happen?"

He gave a slight shrug. "Aye. In theory."

"And how will I know I've changed?"

"You won't be tethered to a body anymore. You will just . . . be."

"I've been there before!" Sheena recalled excitedly. "Sometimes for just a second when we're merging. But it was for a lot longer today when you and I merged with Mi—" She clapped a hand to her mouth before she finished saying his name.

"With your what?" Toni asked. There was a very uncomfortable pause at the table.

"Vibrator. We were experimenting," McRae blurted. It was a spur of the moment effort to keep the truth hidden, and everyone looked at him. "What? I'm sure Toni knows you have one."

"She does now."

"See? They're not the only couple who have been experimenting with merging, Toni," Miles said, and it made her giggle.

Sheena cleared her throat. "Can we get back on topic?"

"Who knows if changing between forms is even a possibility?" Miles glanced at her before picking up his fork. "No warden merger has managed to do it as of this moment. Maybe it's possible for someone who's survived a data-wave exchange without brain damage, like you have, Sheena. But even if it *was* a possibility, we couldn't tell you how to disperse your corporeal body. If you want to go down that road, then it's probably a matter of practice. And if you manage to make it happen . . . then there's no going back."

"What do you mean by *if she wants to go down that road*?" Toni wanted to know. "Who wouldn't want to be able to switch between human and your species?"

"It'll change everything. It'll change what she knows and how she thinks. It'll change her future. It'll change her whole *existence.* She'll have the choice to remain on Earth or to be with us."

Sheena ate absently as all manner of disordered thoughts swirled in her head. Did she want to? If she did, then why? If she didn't, then why not? What frustrated her the most was the unknown. If only she could research the effects, the advantages and disadvantages, and other people's experiences and opinions like she would with any other huge life decision.

Throughout most of lunch, she was tuned out of the conversation, but every time she glanced at McRae, he was looking at her.

After lunch, Toni and Miles left, giving Sheena some time and breathing space to consider her future.

She poured two glasses of wine, and McRae followed her out onto the back balcony. He watched her sip at her drink as she cast her eye over the magnificent view she had over the dam and ranges. She felt peaceful for the first time in months.

"When *are* you leaving?" she asked.

"There isn't a deadline. It's my own decision. And time is irrelevant to me."

"You know I'm in love with you, Eric McRae, Park Ranger."

He gave a grin and leaned across the table to entwine his fingers with hers. "You share that emotion with me each time we merge. And I have shared it back, although I'm not sure you understand what I share when we're merged."

"Usually not. I understood everything today."

McRae nodded. "Aye. Today was different."

Again, Sheena drank in the summer vista of the valley. She savoured the loud chirping from a thousand cicadas in the trees, the chorus of birdsong. The air was pure; the water was pure. Earth was on the brink of reform. This was her dream, her simple life amongst the native flora and fauna. Again, she could feel McRae's eyes on her, and she met his gaze.

"So will you stay on Earth with me? Will you marry me and have children with me and grow old with me?"

He gave a slight frown. "Are you not even going to see if you're able to change forms first before you make a decision?"

"You know I can. I did it earlier today, and I know you're aware it happened. It's not a question of can I—it's a question of *will* I. So are you willing to stay here on Earth with me for another sixty years?"

McRae sat back with his glass and took a long swallow as he looked her serious face over. "If that's what will make you the happiest. Aye, I'll stay here with you and grow old with you."

Sheena nodded, firmly holding his gaze. "Then you've made it easy for me to make a decision."

McRae gave the slightest of smiles. "I thought I knew you, Miss Sheena. I really thought you'd choose to be one of us. I thought you wouldn't be able to resist the allure of existing in all dimensions. I thought you'd want to experience first contact with new species and help bring planets back from the edge of ruin. I was hoping you'd want to exist eternally with my conscience. I was hoping you'd want to exist eternally with *me*."

Sheena finished her wine off and slid onto his lap, giving his full lips a long and lingering kiss. She pulled back and looked into his deep blue eyes.

"You *do* know me, McRae. Because that's exactly what I've decided to do."

About the Author

NJ van Vugt is a self-confessed sci-fi geek, paranormal enthusiast, and fantasy fanatic. Did I mention sci-fi geek? In a previous life she was an editor, has been writing science fiction and fantasy since the dawn of time, but has recently skewed off on an erotica tangent to see where it would take her. NJ van Vugt is now unleashing her powers of titillation on the unsuspecting public. Will she succeed in inspiring the minds of her readers? Stay tuned.

www.ingramcontent.com/pod-product-compliance
Lightning Source LLC
LaVergne TN
LVHW010114170826
845678LV00012B/2411

9781487440749